ATRO CITY

The flood

ANI TALWAR

ISBN: 1540435024
ISBN 13: 9781540435026
Library of Congress Control Number: 2016919275
CreateSpace Independent Publishing Platform
North Charleston, South Carolina

TABLE OF CONTENTS

This is a book that will tell a story about another book, which was written in innocence, found with a purpose, and hidden with will. Said book is more formally known as "The Book of Wishes," but it was written as a journal of answers.

1875

"**Charles Edward Bowl!**"

Jumping off his bed, the blond boy hurried to hide his storybook. He stilled as he heard the wooden stairs creak. The call hadn't been from his strict mother, Victoria; this was the voice of Lizzie, his friend! He hurried to pick up his garments from the floor, and then he hastily straightened as Lizzie pushed the door open.

"Oh, Charles! I request that you answer, and yet you leave me to greet silence!" Lizzie walked through the door and perched on his bed, which lay along the wall to the right of the room. Charles sighed, smiling nevertheless. He rolled his eyes as he felt his socks hit his back. Of course, she would notice the one thing he had missed.

"But, oh, Elizabeth," he returned, speaking in the same posh manner as she had, "I request you to lay your sweet eye on sense. For your person was not met by silence but rather my mother, who opened the door for you." Lizzie rolled her eyes at his imitation of her speech. "And may I ask," he carried on with a grin, "what is so wrong about being greeted with silence? I find him a faithful companion. He always remains, even after every song finishes."

"Well," she replied, walking to his desk against the opposite wall. She glanced out the window above it and then busied herself by putting his drawing pencils back into his pot. "It is not so much a wrong but a bore. You leave me in his presence so very often that we first became old friends, then close companions, and now I fear we are quite tired of each other. It seems all he

1

wants to do is be silent, whilst I long for a good conversation with my friend Charles."

Pausing, Charles searched his mind for a suitable response, but he found none. He sighed, defeated. As always, she won their little verbal competition. She was a great writer like that: she was never lost for words. She smiled triumphantly as he bowed, showing his defeat.

"Alas," he sighed, "I am no match for the majestic Lizzie."

The girl laughed, her dark waves shaking as she did so. "You can never beat me," she said, a smirk gracing her face. It curled into a frown as a gust of wind blew from the window. It was accentuated by the draught that seeped in through the bricks of Charles's room.

"It's an unusually cold night evening tonight," Lizzie remarked, going over to look out the window. Looking to either side, she could see the brick walls that made up the houses, which were cramped side by side almost the whole way down the road. Looking down, she could see the top of the window below and smell the pie that was baking in the adjoining room.

"And I'm sure the all-knowing Elizabeth has the answer as to why." Charles smiled, going over to join her at the window. She wrinkled her nose at his use of her full name. Nevertheless, she pointed over the tops of the cramped houses that lined the other side of the road and over the horizon.

Squinting against the setting sun, Charles and Lizzie could make out the silhouette of the famous chimneys. They belonged to the biggest factory their town owned.

"Have you noticed," Lizzie said, walking away from the window, "that every summer, when the factory works the most, old Mrs. Edger starts having her problems again?"

Charles sighed—Lizzie and her mysteries. He looked up as he heard a shout of "Watch!" from the window above. He ducked in just in time to miss the bucket of waste that was sent downwards. Wrinkling his nose, he joined Lizzie on the red throw that covered the middle of the cold stone floor.

"Enlighten me," he said. "Why does the pattern of Mrs. Edger's problems mean anything?"

Lizzie's brows furrowed. From the look on her face, Charles could tell she was gathering up one of her many ideas so she could explain it. From the folds of her dress, she pulled out the notebook and pen that always accompanied her wherever she went. As she flicked through the pages, he caught glimpses of her scrawling writing.

Lizzie, desperate to write a whole book someday, had taught herself the basics of writing from any old letters she could get her hands on. Charles's father, being a postman, had taught Charles how to read, and Charles had helped Lizzie learn. Now, whenever she travelled, she wrote her ideas down, in the hopes of writing a book.

Finding her page, Lizzie held it up for Charles to see. It was a rough sketch of a factory. From its two chimneys, smoke rose out in ribbons. Next to it, he saw a crude drawing of Mrs. Edger with smoke going into her nose.

"I believe," Lizzie explained, "that the factory itself is the very cause of Mrs. Edger's problems."

Charles bent his eyebrows. "And you are convinced of this...because of the smoke?" he asked. As close as he and Lizzie were, her ways still confused him sometimes. Unlike her, Charles had no intention of writing. Instead, he longed to sit within the trees and talk to the birds whilst sketching their fine forms. Because he lived in a cramped town, Charles rarely went outside its borders and into the country. That sort of thing was for the rich. The few times he had ventured past the walls of the town, he had loved every minute of it. However, he lived in a tall stone house cramped in between hundreds of other stone houses. He smiled; he still had Lizzie, who was waiting for his thoughts to run their course so she could explain.

"Sorry," he said, shaking his head. "I'm all ears."

She smiled, bouncing on her heels. "I think it is exactly the smoke that hinders Mrs. Edger." She sighed, wondering how to explain. "Do you ever notice how when the factory season comes and the smoke hangs low, the air feels...thick?" she asked.

Charles cast his mind back to last summer, when the heat had come. The air *had* felt thick and strange. He nodded.

She leaned forwards, in complete explaining mode. "Well, what if this air *thickness* is what makes Mrs. Edger troubled. Maybe she isn't used to this thick air. Maybe because the air isn't as...fine as it usually is, it doesn't pass through her...pipes...as easily, and that causes Mrs. Edger trouble." She looked at

Charles intently, eager for an opinion on her theories. Slowly, he nodded. There was an essence of logic in what she was thinking.

"Think about it," she continued eagerly, "Mrs. Edger's problems really only started about four years ago."

Charles furrowed his eyebrows. "Wasn't the big factory made four years ago?" he mused.

Lizzie smirked triumphantly, and Charles realised he had just proven her point for her.

"Exactly," she agreed.

"So what do you propose?" he asked. "Take down the factories to save Mrs. Edger?"

"Factories! Saving lives! Golly, you are having grown-up talks indeed!"

Both children jumped up, and Lizzie hurried to smooth her dress. Though she hated dresses, she took care to look as formal and neat as she could in the presence of Charles's mother, Victoria.

Victoria looked kindly at Charles, but he saw the disapproving look in her eyes as they flickered towards Lizzie. After a period of silence, she handed a paper to Charles. "You and Elizabeth can go to the shop for me" was all she said, and then she walked out the room.

The room was silent for a few moments before both Charles and Lizzie burst out laughing.

"She hates me so much!" Lizzie laughed. She retrieved her pen and book off the floor, and together, the two children made their way out.

"I wonder *why* your mother hates me so much…" Elizabeth mused as they travelled—Elizabeth skipping, and Charles walking—down the street. Every so often, they would have to jump over the river of waste running down the centre of the street.

"She doesn't so much dislike as disapprove of you," Charles replied absentmindedly. He was longingly gazing through the gates placed in a gap between houses, through which he could see the huge upper-class houses. He saw the bakery not far through the gates. The day he was able to scrounge up enough money for one of those cakes, well, that *would* be the day.

"I know *that*, Charlie!" Elizabeth sighed, giving him a poke in the shoulder. "What I want to know is *why*!"

4

Charles shook his head, rubbing the offended shoulder with his hand. "You know full well, Lizzie, that I cannot be of any use there," he said. "I don't know why my mother disapproves of you, any more than I know how to write the words in the alphabet." Because although Lizzie could write, Charles could only read. He had tried to learn to write but his hand had hurt from holding his pen so tightly and he had instead learned that sketching was far easier and taken that up instead, and not learned to write.

"They are letters, Charles, not words." She sighed, having expected such an answer. Though it was not her greatest concern, she did wonder why Charles's mother harboured such a venomous dislike of her.

"How is your father then?" Lizzie asked. Charles's father, being a post-man, often spent his time in the upper-class village or travelling with the richer men. Despite this, he had made a fast friend and admirer of Elizabeth. She longed to spend her days travelling and on "a jolly smashing adventure," as she put it.

"My father, as always, is in good health," replied Charles, pulling Elizabeth out of the path of another bucketful of waste being dropped.

"Such dirt!" Elizabeth exclaimed, hoisting her dress up to avoid spoiling it.

"Mmm," Charles said, for he was deep in thought. He wondered. He didn't know why his mother disliked Lizzie, but maybe he could remember when it all might have started.

He remembered the day he had met Lizzie. It had been the start of many sporadic meetings that had finally led him to be her close companion.

ᴬ

A boy hurriedly ran down the concrete-and-wood stairs. Tripping on the bottom one, he caught hold of the railing and grandly swung himself down.

"Now you be careful, Charles," the boy's mother said from the top of the stairs. He grinned cheekily but nodded. He heard his father's heavy footsteps as he took the stairs two at a time to meet Charles.

"And you keep close to your father, mind," his mother said, turning her sharp gaze towards his father, who paused on the stairs, turning to nod at his wife.

"'Aste! 'Aste!" the nine-year-old Charles shouted in excitement; he couldn't wait to leave. His parents glanced down at him with soft smiles; his mother made to speak, but she was interrupted.

"Haste," a voice said from behind Charles.

Charles, along with his parents, turned to the arch in front of the stairs that gave way to the open street. Standing near the side was a young girl, whose hair was a mess of waves and who was wearing a small maid's dress, looking at the family.

"It's *haste*; not '*aste*," she repeated once more, though nervously now that she had the attention of the boy's parents as well.

"Well, yes, thank you for that," the little boy's mother said stiffly, coming down to place a hand on the boy's back. She eyed the Peter Roy's House on the small badge sewn on the girl's dress. It was a requirement that the children living in Peter Roy's House wore a badge to "warn" people that they were from there. Charles's mother knew that place, and only children whose parents had deemed them unfit were sent there. Only the lowest of lowest children, who had no hope for living in a polite society, lived in that house.

⅄

But of course, young Charles didn't know that, and because his mother was eager to keep his mind innocent and free from the more despairing qualities of Victon, the place Charles lived, she hadn't told him. And so it was that despite his mother's thinly concealed hatred towards the children of Peter Roy's House, Charles found himself becoming fast friends with the lonely little girl who lived in the big old building down the dark alley of Victon.

Now, as Charles walked alongside his friend to the shop his mother had sent them to, Charles looked at the badge on Lizzie's dress and wondered why it had made his mother hate Lizzie. He wondered why the badge made *everyone* hate Lizzie.

"Oh, Charles, do look!" Lizzie called from somewhere behind him. He realised she had stopped and was looking eagerly in one of the polished windows of the shop. He joined her at the glass, placing his hands beside his face so he didn't have to contend with the reflections of the street.

Inside the shop, he saw books. Books on any subject he could imagine. But he could see what had caught Lizzie's fancy: almost shrouded in darkness near the back of the shop was a small journal. It was brown, with a small rectangular area on the front where one could write the title, and it was thick with yellow pages.

"Come on," he said, pushing her into the shop. "Have a peek."

Hesitantly, she shuffled into the shop, knowing that she would not be able to afford the book but wanting to see just what could have been. Gingerly, she picked it up and turned it over to look at the back cover, which had the same smooth brown cover as the front of the book. She flicked through the pages, admiring the quality, and let herself think what it would be like to own such a thing.

From somewhere left of them, they dimly heard the owner of the shop walk in.

"One day," Lizzie said, "I will buy this book."

She spoke with such conviction that Charles had to admire her. For the book cost a whole five pounds, and any realistic girl of her status would know that to have that much money was a mere dream. However, Charles wasn't quick to doubt Lizzie; his friend had proved herself successful before.

"Hey!" Both children started at the address from the owner who had entered and was bent over her walking stick.

"Madam!" Charles said quickly, standing in front of Lizzie and shielding the badge on her dress from view. "We were admiring this lovely journal you have," he said politely, bowing to the woman. "My friend here was saying how she'd like to buy it one day."

The owner looked over Charles's shoulder and eyed Lizzie, who shrank backwards slightly under the gaze.

"By all means," the woman said, "buy it, if you have enough money."

Lizzie looked down and then held the book out to the woman. Lizzie was defeated; she knew she didn't have the money.

"I say," the woman said, taking pity on the small girl, "I will keep the book for one week. If you can come up with *honest* money to pay for it, you can have it. Take more than one week, and I will put it back on the shelves for other people to buy."

Lizzie looked up at her with hope and glee. "Thank you, kind madam!" she said. She took Charles's arm. "Haste, Charles!" she said. "Let us go and find some work!"

If only it were that easy. The duo walked all day and into the afternoon and failed to find sufficient employment. By evening, the dejected pair walked back towards the shop. Only they had forgotten to do the rest of the shopping. Forgotten to tell Mrs. Bow of their whereabouts. Forgotten that she hated Elizabeth.

As he walked along next to Lizzie, Charles felt some sympathy for his friend, who somehow became the constant recipient of everyone's hatred. He could only think of two things about Lizzie that could make people hate her so. The first was the badge on her dress, which seemed to turn people away for a reason that had never been explained to Charles, and it didn't matter that Lizzie was good, the badge, for some reason, made everyone think bad of her before she even opened her mouth. The second was the concealed notebook, which was always hidden in the folds of her dress. Poor children shouldn't know how to write; writing was a skill for the rich. Lizzie knew how to write, and Charles couldn't tell if people hated her more for rebelling against the norm or rather feared her for it.

However, Charles reasoned that if people knew what Lizzie speculated about in her notebook, they might do more than hate her. Her notebook was filled with notes on how the factories did more harm than good, how they were not a blessing to workers but rather the cause of their redundancy. She wrote about the war she had heard about, about how it wasn't an adventure. But more dangerously, she wrote about the answers to these problems.

She wrote about little cans with clean air in them that people like Mrs. Edger could use when the air got dirty. She wrote about ways people could learn to write themselves with minimal help and therefore earn their own livings without factories. She wrote about the simple ways that lower-class people could learn to do math and manage their finances so there would be no need for loans. Her notebook held the kinds of things that governments tried to hide from the public so that morale stayed high and soldiers kept volunteering. The kinds of things the rich didn't teach the poor so they would still come crawling back for jobs.

She didn't write about these things because she was a genius. Charles scoffed. Lizzie was far from a genius. However, she was poor and lower class. No one bothered to hide his or her disgust from the lower class. They were illiterate and could not act on any of what they heard. Except Lizzie could. Lizzie could write, and if she achieved her dream and wrote a book, Charles could only imagine the truths she would reveal in it. So yes, in a way, Lizzie was dangerous. But it was more her notebook that held the real dangers.

Which is why when they returned to the shop to find a policeman reading Lizzie's notebook, which she must have dropped on the way, they didn't stop to answer questions. They didn't stop to see how many other men were there for Lizzie's arrest. They didn't stop to see the injured owner of the shop.

They ran.

2029

If I fall asleep now, nobody can blame me.

It's ridiculous for them to expect us to stay awake through the same speech about the book year after year.

"The book could reply to you if you talked to it, and it could grant wishes, but it has only one wish left to give..." Blah, blah, blah. The form teacher droned on.

What rubbish! Wishes and spells! That's the stuff of fairy tales, not of reality. If such things existed, then Fun City would have been put right years ago! I would happily walk out of the classroom right now, but the people of Fun City are here to evaluate our school's education standard, and they disapprove of us already as it is.

To be fair, we don't like them either, but at least we have a good reason. (Unlike them!)

The mutual dislike between our two cities runs a long way back. Sixty-two years to be exact, as Julie reminds me. There was a time when the people of our city and Fun City got along. We all used to live in one big (mostly) happy city called Unistate. However, people started getting sick, and doctors couldn't figure out why. A group of what is now our grandparents did their research and found that the illnesses were caused by the ever-increasing pollution levels.

Prior to this, the group had already been campaigning against the pollution levels but only on a small scale. After our grandparents found out people were getting sick because of pollution, a small group decided to speak out and protest on a larger scale. Most of the people of Unistate, including the government, refused to see sense. (Which is why they were—in my opinion—so stupid.)

The prime minister threatened to exile the antipollution group if they didn't stop. The group didn't stop.

On the outskirts of Unistate was a derelict district with decrepit houses. The government exiled the group of more than one hundred protestors to the derelict district as punishment for the group not stopping their protests.

To rub salt in their wounds, the district was christened Atro City. (It was meant to sound like *atrocity*; the Government did like to think themselves capable of humour after all.) The people of Unistate rechristened what was left of their city Fun City (to poke fun at us, methinks). So, in retaliation, our grandparents shunned the Unistate's, or what was now known as Fun City's, form of government and elected a mayor instead of a prime minister.

Sixty-two years and two generations later, we are a thriving city with our own schools, hospital, and mayor.

Now, our city is better equipped than it was sixty-two years ago; we have developed skills and had training. We have learned how to hunt for our own food when Fun City blocks our supply and trade for random reasons. We have developed the ability to fight and use weapons, such as knives, axes, and bows and arrows. We can now defend ourselves when Fun City haters attack us.

And our generation is the best.

They call our generation the golden generation. By *they*, I mean our parents, who want to make other parents know how good we are. It's like the competition of who can embarrass his or her child the most. (Which, in my opinion, my mother wins every time.)

But, you know, we are a pretty awesome generation (if I do say so myself). The first generation was our grandparents, who were exiled from Fun City. They had very little experience of living on their own means and used out-of-the-box thinking to survive.

The next generation was their children, or our parents; they inherited all the clever tricks from their parents, developed cleverer tricks of their own, and established trade links with surrounding villages.

Then came our generation. Equipped with two generations of wisdom and tricks, we have it made. We can make things, hunt, and fight. If any Fun City idiot tries to attack us, we can show them who's boss.

Which is probably why no one from Fun City attacks us anymore.

For all their wisdom and education, the teachers still find it necessary to harp on at us with the same dumb story of that mythical book. You know, I can see why some people in Fun City think we are stupid. With myths like the talking book (and the fact that our grandparents believe them) it does look like we are a bit odd. And apparently, if the lesson I'm in now says anything, our parents mean to pass on the oddness.

"So, Kayla, who made the first wish from the book?" Mr. Jonses looked at me from over his spectacles. I had almost fallen asleep on my desk. From behind me, Mackenzie Dry giggled; I knew she was making fun of me.

Mackenzie Dry is my archenemy. She looked like any other girl, with brown hair and grey eyes. But I guess evil can take many forms.

I mentally prodded myself to say something. "Uh…" I should have said nothing.

"Charles Edward Bow," Julie whispered from next to me, and I stammered, "Charles Edward Bow?"

Mr. Jonses grunted suspiciously but took my correct answer.

"And the second?" he asked.

I sighed with relief; this one was easy. "No one knows."

That was the bit about this legend that made me sceptical to believe in it. If this book was so rare, then why did no one know who used the second wish? Why was it such a mystery?

The bell for the end of lesson rang. We got up to make our way to self-defence class.

"How could you not remember? They've been telling us these names since we were six!" Julie hissed as we walked out of the classroom after the lesson had finished.

"I've been more focused on the *real* stuff they have to teach us," I replied. She glared at me in response, but I knew she wasn't really angry about my not caring. She was used to Terry (you will meet him later) and I scorning the beliefs of our grandparents. What had annoyed her was the fact that I had not paid attention during such an important class that was even being assessed. Sometimes Julie can be a little bit of an over-the-top perfectionist.

Julie Stotes, short for Julianna Lily Stotes, was my close friend at school. She had blond waves and blue eyes, and when she smiled, she got little dimples under her eyes. She was the complete opposite to my dark hair and brown eyes, which turned black when I got angry. Julie may look like a teeny tiny little doll, but trust me she could be terrifying when she wanted to be.

Remember what I said about our generation being able to fight? Well, it didn't come naturally for all of us (cough—Mackenzie—cough). We had to be trained as fighters. We were trained in shooting, throwing, and close-action fighting.

We had our training in the same area where we ate lunch, which was why we didn't suffer from children bunking off and hiding in the food courts.

The food court/fighting ground started off with a sheltered area, under which there were a few picnic benches. Outside the sheltered area, there was a concrete space. This was also dotted with picnic benches, but there was a circular clearing in the centre that was used for class. The whole area was surrounded with greenery, which hid us well from the main road, which ran on the right and behind the shrubs.

We sat down on a dry bench and looked eagerly at Mr. Bright, our teacher.

"All right, gather around," Mr. Bright yelled. I don't think anyone's ever told him about this great thing called talking quietly. "We'll be learning a new manoeuvre called the Fear Twist. It isn't a move meant to harm, because you shouldn't actually use your various weapons unless absolutely necessary. This move is purely meant to scare your opponent so he or she runs rather than fights."

"Why would someone *not* want to fight?" Reagon asked.

Reagon Saunders was Mackenzie's sidekick. Together, they made Tweedle Dumb and Tweedle Dumber. In all fairness, they aren't that silly; I just don't like them. For one, they make fun of me at every chance they get, and for two, well, I just don't like them.

They both specialise in close-quarter combat like me, and they like to make sure everyone thinks they are better than me. So, of course, I make it a point to prove that *I'm* better at every turn I get.

Mr. Bright pulled out a throwing knife and demonstrated the move. He feigned a strike to the left and then immediately bent down and struck to the right, but he purposefully missed the dummy opponent.

"The purpose here is not to strike but to demonstrate how quick you are, and..."

He carried on the demonstration for about five minutes before dividing us into pairs to practise the move.

"Seems like a good defence move," Julie said as I repeated the move for her to scrutinise. "You're doing it perfectly." She sighed and pulled out her own dagger to show me how she did the move. After a few corrections, she was right on track.

Soon after we had all gotten the hang of it, Mr. Bright decided he would go one-on-one with some students for practice. He looked at me for some time and finally announced that he wouldn't pick me as I wasn't wearing my underarmour. (It's the vest we have to wear so it won't hurt if we get stabbed. It's very dangerous not to wear it.) So he picked Mackenzie.

"This ought to be good, don't you think, Kay?" Terry said to me with a grin.

"Don't call me Kay." I smiled and grimaced at the same time. I do not like being called Kay. Which was, of course, why Terry insisted on calling me that. I wasn't allowed to say one bad word about any teacher or rugby player, but he was allowed to blatantly disobey me.

Julie grinned at him from the other side of me and said, "If only there was popcorn." We all had to stifle giggles.

Terry Smithe was one of the only males in our year who also specialised in close-up combat. Most of the others took archery. Like me, Terry took both. He had brown hair and brown eyes and freckles all over his nose, to the point that when he smiled, his nose was lost under all of them.

Mackenzie and Mr. Bright stood facing each other. Mr. Bright counted down, and the fight started. Mr. Bright faked left and stabbed right, but Mackenzie rolled left and stabbed up. Mr. Bright defended and kicked the blade out of her hand. She ducked as he made a forwards strike, and she swept her blade off of the floor, curving it up so it would theoretically cut his side as she came up. He faked left and struck right once more, but Mackenzie was waiting till the last moment so she could use his momentum to bring him down.

She was just about to strike when something fell on her bare arm. A yellowish drop of water made a small hiss as it touched her arm, and Mackenzie winced. She looked down at her arm with shock and disgust. We realised almost too late that Mr. Bright hadn't noticed and was still striking. Instantly, Jamie, the assistant tutor, stepped in and stopped Mr. Bright.

Mr. Bright looked somewhat confused, but then another drop fell from the sky and right on his nose. He hissed as the drop landed and then shouted, "Acid rain! Everyone get inside!"

At lunch, all the children from school stood in the large conservatory and watched the faintly yellow rain fall.

"So much for a game of football at lunch," one of the older children, Jonathan, complained.

"It's all because of those polluting morons at Fun City," Reagon moaned, and I have to admit she was actually right. (However, if you ever tell her, I will flatly deny ever saying such a thing. You have been warned.)

Mrs. Johns came out to announce the end of lunch. She held a piece of plain paper out in the rain. After only six drops, the paper turned the deepest shade of red. That was not good.

I had geography and art next, which were horrible. We had planned to do various activities outside for both subjects, and now because of the acid rain, they were cancelled. When it was time to go home, people ran with their umbrellas out. Umbrellas did not provide much cover for long.

So it was just great when I found I had left my umbrella at home. Acid rains were a norm in Fun City, thanks to pollution. Acid rains were very rare in Atro City, but recently, they seemed to be on the rise.

My mum was there to pick me up so we could cycle home together.

"Cycle faster!" my mother shouted through the rain as we tried to cycle home as quickly as we could. I had my jumper pulled over my head so I could stay as dry as possible, but it didn't work.

I'm just glad it wasn't my favourite blue one, or Fun City would have had some serious trouble on their hands.

As we left our bikes under the porch and went inside, my mum took a piece of paper and held it out in the rain, just as my teacher had.

Five drops. That's all it took before it turned the deepest shade of red.

"The rain is getting stronger," she said, herding me inside.

It rained heavily for the rest of the afternoon. Later in the evening, Dad came home from work. It turned out he had forgotten his umbrella as well. The cloth of his tie had reacted to the acid rain and turned an amazing shade of orange in places. (Why only his tie was affected, I don't know.)

All this rain made me angry. It wasn't fair that the people of Fun City could have all the fun in the world and not care. How did they deal with acid rain? Well, whatever way they dealt with it, it wasn't fair that we had to as well.

I actually remember once when the people of Atro City wrote to Fun City and asked them to pollute less after there was a spell of acid rain that lasted for almost a week. They didn't stop polluting. Oh no! Their solution was to attack us. Of course, they hugely underestimated us. They attacked when my friends and I were walking home from school.

I'm quite proud to say I actually took two bad guys down. One of them tried to punch me, but I took his arm and used his momentum to push him forwards and past me. He ended up stumbling forwards and right into my good friend, who was known as Tall Pole. (If you ever visit us, make sure to look for the small nose print on the pole.)

The second guy could fight better, but even though I was only twelve, I knew more sneaky tricks. He had a hammer with him for some reason and tried to whack me on the head. I kicked him in the hand and punched down on the inside of his elbow, so his arm bent inwards and towards his face.

Basically, I made him hit himself in the head with his own hammer.

By this time, most of the guys had been beaten back. There was only one left. However, he was the one with a real gun. He pointed it at us and made us stand still. It was my own mother who took him down. She saw me and a guy with a gun, and what did she do? She approached from behind, and she whacked him over the head with her purse, of course. (She carried some heavy stuff in the purse, I guess.)

Since then, I have never complained when my mother made me carry a heavy purse with me when I went out on my own.

But I do complain when she wakes me up at six thirty every morning. Like she did twenty minutes ago. She likes to pull the blankets completely off my bed and let me freeze till I wake up. Such love.

I got out of bed (stone cold) and made my way downstairs to the kitchen. After I had eaten, I went back upstairs to my bedroom to get changed. Just as I was about to go back downstairs to leave for school, my phone beeped. "Look outside. Julie. <3"

I picked up my bag from my bed and walked to the window, undid the curtains, and looked outside, into the back garden. I almost choked in horror.

The rain was almost a sickly yellow. It rained relentlessly on the vegetation in our garden, which was slowly turning pale and dying.

"Dad, you might want to see this," I said shakily.

"Yes, I have seen it," he yelled from downstairs.

"These Fun City people have gone too far this time," I heard my grandmother say as she slowly made her way downstairs. We called her Grammie, and she seemed to like the title.

Acid rain may not seem like much to you guys reading, but it was a big issue, and a bad issue too. Not only was it a stark reminder of the amount of pollution (which I hope you care about), but it also affected health and our plants, which were important to us as we didn't like to produce things in factories but instead grew things ourselves. To put it simply, if things carried on, we would have very little food.

"Darling, come get your coat," my mother yelled from downstairs.

I ran down the stairs and through the hallway to the front door. "Mum, look outside," I said as she unlocked and opened the front door. The sight that greeted us was dire.

From ground level, we could really see how fast the rain was *still* falling. Acid-rain spells were dangerous but usually didn't last this long.

Mum was going to drive me to school today. In Atro City, we used electric-solar hybrid cars. They polluted less. We only used them as a last resort or if we were going somewhere far away; that way, we polluted as little as possible. As I put my seat belt on, my mobile phone buzzed. I had two text messages, one from Julie and another from Terry.

"Kayla, have you seen the rain!" the text from Julie read.

"Fun City has really done it now! Look at the bloody rain," Terry wrote.

"What's going to happen if the rain keeps up?" I asked Mum.

She did not answer; she was removing a sleeve of testing paper from the dashboard. Then she murmured, "We could lose an awful lot."

She rolled the window down and held out the piece of paper, doing the familiar experiment to test the severity of the acid rain. It turned a fiery shade of red, to the point that it almost looked black.

Both of us looked at the testing paper in dismay. The rain was getting stronger. Through the silence, my mum's mobile phone rang loud and clear. Mum picked it up and grimly agreed to whatever the speaker was saying. It was as if she had been expecting the news for some time.

She looked back at me. "The mayor has called a meeting."

1967

"The prime minister has called a meeting."

Lily looked up in shock at her friend. Melanie Walters stood at the door of their "meet" holding a formal envelope in her hand. The Meet was the name given to the building that Lily and her friends often met up in.

"You're joking," Lily said, her dark eyes narrowing in shock. "He wouldn't!"

Melanie shook her head, her blond waves bobbing around her. "I'm not," she replied, handing Lily the envelope. "Read it for yourself."

Taking the envelope, Lily read the letter within.

Dear Mrs. Walters,

As you know, a protest group has recently surfaced. They have caused much trouble and disruption to the good people of Unistate.

As we are unaware of the protesters' identities, we are holding one-on-one meetings with every citizen of the state to see whether we can find out more. I hope you and your family can attend your allocated slot on May 21 at ten o'clock.

Yours truly,

Prime Minister Lennon

The prime minister, as a sign of authenticity, had signed the bottom of the paper personally.

Lily bit her lip nervously as she folded the letter back into the envelope.

Lily and her friends (the oldest of whom was only twenty-three) had been protesting incognito against the pollution in Unistate for over a year now.

They had had little success at first, and so it came as a surprise when all of a sudden, people started paying attention to what they had to say. It seemed their message was spreading and gaining momentum.

Then it got complicated. The group of activists had gathered in their meet on Sunday afternoon as usual. However, instead of being filled with the buzz of happy discussions, the meet had been a subdued event.

That morning, someone had posted a letter under the door. The letter directed the protesters to reduce the scale of their campaigning. It said that so long they did that, the prime minister would turn a blind eye to the fact that his own nephew was part of the group. If they didn't, and it became known who and what the group was all over the city, then the prime minister would take action—and it wouldn't be good.

"I'm sure you understand," the letter had said, "it cannot be known that the prime minister's own kin disagrees with his ways of running the city. It would cause all sorts of chaos and not to mention riots. So if you keep the campaign on a small scale, then I won't tell the prime minister the truth about his nephew. If you don't…well, I think the implications of that are clear."

Whether fake or not, the letter had scared them. Firstly, whoever wrote it knew the location of the protesters' meet, something they thought they had kept a complete secret. Secondly, the person knew their identities. For fear of trouble, they had not even told their parents what they were doing.

So far, the group had only used anonymous methods to spread their message. They used fake names online and wore elaborate masks and makeup when forced to talk face to face with those who weren't part of the group. They only talked to those who didn't know them personally to avoid detection. They had taken great care to hide their identities.

It was a shock to find one person who knew all of them.

Lily was brought out of her reverie by the shaking of the wooden floor at meet.

"Ugh, boys are so loud!" Melanie moaned, having also felt the shaking.

All the members of the group had keys, which allowed them through the gates and into the back entrance of the meet. However, they had to climb up some way to get to it, and when the boys of the group climbed, it made miniearthquakes through the room.

The meet was a hybrid of tree house and a mansion's top floor. On one of the roads at the back of the city, right near the forest, there had once stood a grand mansion, but the head of the household had been a lonely man, and when he died, the house had fallen into disrepair. Later, a group of children had found the ruins, which had a huge tree growing straight through the middle of the house. After climbing, they had found some of the top floor intact. They had strengthened the floor and added walls around the tree trunk and converted it into a tree house. After they had grown out of it, it had been left for someone else to find.

Years later, a group of friends, soon to become the protest group, walked through the grounds behind the mansion. They had all been given keys to the allotment, as they were doing summer work on the grounds. In the midst of their work, Melanie had found the tree house. It could be accessed by climbing the tree and going in through the back window. However, you could also access it from the main road. All you had to do was walk up the garden to the ruins and make your way up what was left of the stairs.

One year later, once the protest group had formed, the friends decided to make use of their keys and use the tree house as their meet. They decided to use the back entrance, as there was less chance they would be seen entering the house. Also, if anyone had to knock on the door, they could then tell the person was an intruder.

However, as Melanie and Lily could feel the floor shaking, they knew the person about to enter was one of the Ecos, as they called themselves. True to their predictions, Josh Peterson promptly fell through the window.

"Gosh," he moaned. "We need a bigger window."

Lily laughed, helping him up.

"Or you could just stop growing," she retorted.

Josh's height was a standing joke between the Ecos. He had had a growth spurt one day, and it seemed as if he hadn't stopped growing since. The blond boy helped himself to a biscuit from the table by the left wall.

"I fill think ee ould et igger indow," he managed between mouthfuls.

"Chew your food!" Melanie reprimanded, hitting his shoulder. "Then talk."

He dutifully remained silent as he finished his biscuit. Then, his brown eyes wide with mock innocence, he turned to Melanie.

"Do you think I'm a good boy now, Mummy?" he asked, putting on a baby voice.

Unable to help it, Lily burst out laughing. She laughed even more when Melanie pushed Josh, and he fell backwards off the stool he had been perching on.

"Jokes aside," he said from the floor. "I still think we need a bigger window."

Sobering, Lily picked up the envelope from the floor.

"We have bigger issues," she said. "The prime minister has called a meeting."

At once, Josh sat up straight, looking between the two girls.

"Well, that's great!" he said. "If he's asked to talk to us, maybe he has changed his mind about our ideas." He narrowed his eyes. "Or maybe he has found whomever sent us that letter and wants to apologise to us."

Melanie sighed and gestured for Lily to show him the contents.

"That's not even close, Josh," Lily said, handing him the letter. Slowly, he read it.

1875

The countryside was beautiful.

Gone was the constant noise, the stench of filth, and the dropping waste. That lay behind Charles and Lizzie at the end of the cobbled path they had run down so fast. As Charles and Lizzie slowed their pace to a walk, they had a chance to take in the view.

It was almost hard to believe that just a few miles away lay a cramped war-filled town. It was even harder to believe that the war was raging with Blue Sea Bay, that lay a few miles west on the coast.

In front of Lizzie and Charles, the path led down the hill and over to nature knew where. They turned right and off the defined track, walking over the puddles and pebbles. The hill sloped down in steep ridges, and the children found cover under one of those. To their right, the hill sloped up again in steep ridges towards Blue Sea Bay.

Huddling together, they decided to look at what they had. From their shopping they had done for Charles's mother, they had some bread and a few carrots. They also had one whole pound and a small flask of water that they had taken before they left.

That left them with Charles's cloak, Lizzie's badge, a team of policemen on their tail, and a quest to earn five pounds. It didn't help that they were on land directly between Blue Sea Bay and Victon, with no side to claim in the war.

"I am going to write all of this down," Lizzie said once they had checked what they had. Charles looked at her incredulously.

"You have no home, and policemen are after your head, and you are going to *write*?" he asked, not knowing whether to admire her calm or think her mad. She sighed.

"Policemen are troublesome to us, but a home…I didn't have one anyway," she said calmly, and the slight squint to her eye betrayed her slight sadness about the fact, even though she tried to hide it.

"You did," he said quietly. "Once…you did."

For once, she had. She had, or at least he thought she had, a home and two parents and nice toys. But then one day, she had turned up at the children's house with no parents and no recollection of what might have happened. No memory of anything before she was seven. And yet, she had remained optimistic, saying she would learn how to write. She had gone through every book she could find to try and find out where her parents were, but being unable to read before she had met Charles, she had only been able to look through the pictures. A poor girl's parents were not going to be important enough for a hand-drawn picture. So she had found little.

Then she had turned to the police, asking time and time again whether they had any information about her parents, any pictures, anything. But two missing people whom no one remembered and an annoying seven-year-old at their heels made the policemen become bored and angry with her quickly. Although she had left them alone after that, they still remembered her face, which was probably why they were so quick to believe Mrs. Bow's accusations about her.

"Well," Charles said in an attempt to rid himself of the memories, "maybe now you shall find your parents."

Lizzie perked up slightly. Yes, they were stranded and alone, but that's how she had arrived in Victon, so maybe it was fitting that that was how she would leave.

"We could sneak into Blue Sea Bay!" he whispered with excitement. "How jolly it will be if that's where your parents are."

She laughed that shy little giggle, and he felt proud to have created the purpose for it.

"Why, I think Officer Hobs would just find that a right laugh!" she said, and they both laughed, imagining the grumpy man who had told Lizzie outright that he didn't give a pence for her emergency, as he had one of his own that was far more important.

"Yes, that would b—" Charles was cut off by a sickening bang. The ground shook beneath them, and the earth over their heads crumbled dangerously. They shot to their feet, stumbling, and the ground lurched beneath them. Another bang followed, along with the sound of earth splitting apart. A wave of stifling heat passed by them, and together, they turned around.

The bombs had hit home; the war had gone up a level.

Charles darted for the basket with their only food and water in it, Lizzie picked up her dress, and together, they ran. They went south first, their feet taking them back towards Victon out of habit. They saw the policemen at the border and heard the screams of fear in the town and instantly turned the other way. If they went back to Victon, they had no chance of dodging the men and escaping the prisons. At least out here, they had a chance of escaping the bombs.

They ran as fast as their twelve-year-old legs would allow. Pebbles and dust were flying haphazardly everywhere, and it made Lizzie cough. The heat in the air burned Charles's shoulders and made the dry dust hot, hurting Charles's feet as he stepped on it.

They turned their faces away from the wind, hoping to avoid most of the dust. It worked until Lizzie's dress became tangled in her legs, and she fell straight into a deep puddle. She quickly scrambled to her feet, but fell back again as her dress became tangled once more. By the time she managed to stand, she was soaking wet and shivering. Charles only hoped that the nauseating heat would dry her dress fast as they ran away from both Victon and the bomb.

Fortunately, the heat did eventually dry Lizzie's dress, and the two children eventually stopped running and took refuge under the huge branches of an oak tree. Perhaps unfortunately, their run away from the bomb had led them very close to another town: Blue Sea Bay.

Charles wanted get to Blue Sea Bay and then hide the badge on Lizzie's dress and seek refuge in the town, where no one had to know where the children came from, but Lizzie couldn't. Her head hurt, and she felt all "sludgy," as she called it, and so they huddled under the tree, and she fell into a fitful sleep whilst he kept watch.

It soon became apparent that something was wrong. Charles didn't feel tired, and no one had come looking for them, but that was only part of it. As Lizzie slept with her head on his shoulder, Charles could slowly feel her becoming hotter and hotter, and her breathing becoming more laboured. It turned out she hadn't dried fast enough, because if Charles was right (and he thought he was), Lizzie was sick.

The boy felt a surge of anger towards his mother. Lizzie always wore trousers. Sure they were for boys, but they cost less, and she could do more in them—like run! It was because she knew Charles's mother hated her that Lizzie had worn a dress, and now because of it, she was sick.

Next to him, Lizzie shivered, even though the air was warm. Charles sighed; he had nothing to warm her. Slowly, he woke her up.

"Lizzie, let's go into the town," he said gently. He helped her to her feet and noticed how although she tried to hold herself up as if she were fine, she swayed slightly. He caught her arm, and she pulled away a bit.

"I'm fine!" she said, though not unkindly. He let go of her arm but stayed close anyway. Then, at a much slower pace than what either of them would have liked, they made their way to the town.

"It would've been so much easier if you were wearing trousers like you normally do when my mum isn't around," Lizzie winced at Charles's tone as he grumbled. Charles was surprised when Lizzie gave a chuckle that turned into a cough and lifted the bottom of her dress slightly.

"Charles, I *always* wear trousers," she said, revealing the fact that under her dress, she indeed did have trousers on. Charles couldn't help it—he laughed too. Then they set to work changing her troublesome dress into a top. They ripped off the skirt, all three awkward layers. Lizzie and Charles each took a layer. Charles wrapped his around his waist and rolled the water and food into it like a bag, and Lizzie wrapped hers around her shoulders and under one arm, where she had the money. Half of the last layer went into each "bag" to be used as bandages or, in Lizzie's case, as a jumper.

With that done, the duo finally stepped through the gates of the town.

Blue Sea Bay was *nothing* like Victon. There were no cramped houses or narrow streets. The streets were wide, with all sorts of people milling about. The shops had windows the children could see through without squinting, and instead of thin tall cramped houses, the houses were wide and short, with actual gaps between them.

However, whilst Charles took all this in with glee, Lizzie was looking down and trying to put one foot in front of the other. She tried to hide the coughs and the aching of her head, but she felt all shaky. However, she was not going to let anyone know; she was going to earn five pounds, and she was going to keep Charles safe.

The duo walked around the street in awe, until finally, they decided that they really did need to find work if they had any hope of surviving at all.

Slowly, they began to ask around at shops for work. The first lady didn't need help but turned them away kindly, the second man had just closed his shop (why they couldn't imagine) and wouldn't talk, and the third wouldn't let them in because they were so dirty. This trend carried on for most of the day, and the children wondered why it was that people could be so nice and yet so mean at the same time.

Lizzie swayed slightly as they made their way to what seemed like the twentieth shop they had found. This one was taller than the buildings around it; it was a little bakery, with a second floor that housed the shop's owners. Lizzie turned, pretending to admire the view of the sea over the rooftops and down the curving hill, but really, she was hiding her sneezing. Her head hurt as it bobbed slightly, and she almost lost her footing, but she didn't say anything. They needed this work, or they would starve on the streets.

She turned slightly toward the shop, squinting through her tired eyes at the sign she thought she had recognised. She blinked slightly; she couldn't have recognised the sign because she hadn't recognised anything since she was seven. She couldn't because she had no memory to be able to recognise anything. However, as she stood and listened through foggy ears as Charles began to talk with the lady who owned the bakery, she was hit with a dizzying sense of recognition—a taste of cinnamon, and the feel of pastry.

She remembered a child, a parent's hand, a smell of sugar. A hurt hand and a tissue. She had been sick then too.

She?

Lizzie jolted slightly as she realised that she was remembering herself. She had never remembered anything before. The jolt was all it took though. Her head throbbed with the sudden movement, and spots danced in front of her eyes.

"Lizzie!"

She heard a shout from Charles, and that brought her back somewhat, but her eyes were tired, and once more, the dots came forth. She watched as they joined together, and she fell into unconsciousness.

1875

Lizzie was five. She ran beside her mum through the streets of the bay, stopping to wave to the man at the bookshop who looked after her when her parents were away for work.

She giggled in delight as she and her mum neared the bakery. Although Lizzie was sick and felt droopy, she had managed to tidy up the entire living room and make a very nice birthday card for her mummy's friend, and so she was getting a treat: fresh bread, cheese, and banana sandwiches, her favourites.

They walked into the little shop with its flowered walls and glass cabinets holding beautiful treats in them.

"Hi, Aunt Sareen," she sang out to the lady with the wispy brown hair and blue eyes.

Lizzie ran up to the side of the shop where baskets holding bread hung. She could almost imagine the bread rising in the oven.

Then she was in the oven. No. She was outside. But it was so hot. The heat burned her face, and her head felt heavy under the pressure. She ran, but her feet would not go fast enough. And there was Charles, running ahead. He was looking back, shouting "Go!" at her, although she couldn't hear him. He was trying to run back, but his mother held him in place.

She couldn't move. Charles was in front of her and was shouting and trying to save her. However, she couldn't hear anything; the world was scarily silent. Then words seemed to float into her ears, like a song.

"Lizzie," the words said. "Your name is Elizabeth," they said. "Elizabeth S—" But then, the voices stopped, the rest of the world shot into focus, and noise blasted at her.

The bomb was close, the fire was all around her; she ran but not fast enough.

A bang, and she ran faster.

A crash—she was blown off her feet.

She saw the ground coming to meet her. She lifted a hand up, bracing herself. The floor was closer and—

Lizzie woke up with a gasp.

"Lizzie, you're awake!" She turned her head to the side to see Charles sitting by her bed, a look of absolute relief on his face.

Her bed?

She realised as she came fully back to the world of the living that she was in a bed. She was hot and achy, but she definitely felt better than she had before. She sat up slightly, taking in the light-blue walls and wavy green curtains that were swaying in the breeze.

"Where am I?" she managed.

Charles gave her a little smile at that and handed her some water. "Your aunt's house," he answered.

She choked. The water in the glass flew everywhere as her hands went slack, and the water she had drunk went down the wrong pipe. She leaned forwards and into herself as she coughed before finally managing to regain her breath. Charles chuckled. She looked tired and worn out, but Lizzie hadn't changed a bit.

"My *who*?" she demanded once she had gotten her breath back.

"She says she isn't your real aunt, but you used to call her that. You knew her once and called her Aunt—"

"Sareen," Lizzie finished, looking up at him. He raised his eyebrows. She certainly hadn't known that fact yesterday, or the day before, or any day since she was seven and she had woken up in a weird building with no memories.

He looked at her closely, ignoring the darkness under her eyes and the shaking of her hands. He looked at the slight triumph on her face, the tear in her eye. He remembered watching her as she muttered in her fevered sleep. She had said his name and someone else's name too.

"You remember!" he whispered quietly. At her shocked nod, he laughed. "That's great! You remember something!" he said, letting himself do a small dance around the bed. She giggled.

"Charles, sit down!" she said quickly. "Let me tell you everything I saw!"

And although Charles at one time would have questioned her desire to tell him something that she knew, he had learned enough not to underestimate the power of talking. Because he could look on her memories with a new angle, an angle they perhaps needed.

And so he sat there in glee and listened to her talk. She told him of her memories, the bakery, and finally, the dream that ended with the bomb. And afterwards, she eagerly told him about how she was going to write her story down once she got her notebook back. Her dream had helped her realise that there was something a little bit unexplainable in the world, and of course, now she wanted to explain it.

Charles realised as she talked about her plans to write all the answers to everything (yes, everything, as if she thought there was a limit to the questions that could be asked; such a thought from her was ironic, seeing as *she* asked most of the questions that nobody could explain), that she hadn't realised the one thing that had been obvious to him. She was so happy to have remembered something—even though it was only a little—because she hadn't been able to remember anything from before she was seven, but she hadn't seen the obvious.

"Lizzie. Lizzie!" Charles said excitedly, interrupting her. She scowled slightly at him but let him talk. "You fail to realise," he said, "that in your dream, you were walking to this very shop. This means your parents lived in Blue Sea Bay!"

"Yes, bu—" Lizzie stopped, speechless, a feat of which Charles felt immensely proud. He watched with glee as the truth dawned on her face. Here she was in bed whilst her parents may well be only a few short minutes away. For a few minutes, Charles and Lizzie forgot about the police, about the money, and about having to get a job. Both of them stood up eagerly and (after making the bed, because not even Charles could get away from his mother's voice in his head telling him that a made bed was always a clean bed) rushed out the door to find Lizzie's parents.

2029

The last time the mayor called a meeting due to heightened level of pollution, I was three. It turned out I didn't remember the experience very well. If I had, I would have remembered to bring a fan to the meeting. We were slightly boiled because there were so many of us packed in one hall.

Secondly, I would have remembered to bring a megaphone so I could yell, "Excuse me!" to the people in my way.

The main hall was absolutely stuffed with people when I got there with my family. We got there just in time because people had started crowding outside and into that shop that sells TVs so they could see the replay of whatever it was the mayor was planning to say.

The main hall was a large marbled structure. Its domed roof was made out of glass so the inner hall lit up as the sun rose over the horizon. A set of stairs led up to the main doors, with a railing on either side. This was where we temporarily left our bikes to go inside the main room.

We politely made our way to the front so Grammie could take her place in one of the seats. If you remember from what I said earlier about our grandparents, I told you that it was our grandparents who rebelled against the irresponsible actions of Fun City. My very own grandma was one of the rebels. Since the inception of Atro City, my grandmother has held the honour of being a member of the city council. She is always invited to all city meetings as a guest of honour.

Once the last few people had quieted down, Mayor Clinton raised his voice.

"As you all know, the pollution levels of Fun City have reached an all-time high. Their lack of ecofriendliness is the cause of this acid-rain spell. It is time to do something about this."

He gestured to his right, where one of the students from school was sitting on an exercise bike. He began pedalling, and the projector sputtered on and began to project images against the wall.

"Since our banishment, Fun City has conducted many large public events, each of which has caused higher pollution levels than the last."

The projected image flickered till we saw pictures of laughing people under a sky painted with fireworks.

"Their continued use of coal and fossil fuel and complete lack of control of deforestation has led to pollution spreading to neighbouring areas. Our environmental scientists have studied the levels of pollution from Fun City, and they have linked the increase in pollution to the acid rains in Atro City."

The picture flickered once more, and we saw a picture of a man with floppy blond hair. He smiled at the camera as he held up a clipboard with his scientific readings on it.

"We have also deciphered links between the severity of natural disasters and the amount of pollution, such as landslides due to the deforestation."

The picture changed once again to a graph. The projected image was crooked, but we could still make out the title: Rate of rise in natural disasters due to pollution and deforestation.

"If Fun City carries on as they are, the acid rain and disasters will get even worse. It is now clear that we have to take drastic action and try to fix what they have damaged." The projector sputtered once more, and the picture disappeared.

"But why do we have to fix it? It's Fun City's fault!" one of the men shouted out. I vaguely recognised him from Terry's fifth birthday party, so I think it was his uncle.

"Kayla." My mum prodded me. "I don't think I padlocked our bicycles; please go and check."

"What!" I exclaimed. "But I want to hear what they will do."

"I will fill you in later; I just want to make sure the bikes are locked," my mum said stiffly, putting on her business face for good measure.

"Fine." Sulking, I made my way through the hall and out of the front door.

"We have to find this book that holds answers to our…" I could faintly hear the mayor's voice over the rush of the rain.

Outside, I tied the bikes to the railing with the stretchy lock. I pulled my hoodie over my head to stop my hair being singed.

"We need volunteers to mount a mission…" I heard the mayor's voice faintly through the partially open entrance door.

"Dumb thing…just stretch!" I muttered as I wrestled with the chain to go across the wheels of my mum's bike as well as my dad's bike and my bike. "I need to hear! Ah!" The chain unravelled, and I fell backwards.

Great, now I was wet back *and* front. I gave the chain one last pull and heard as it gave a satisfying click.

I quickly ran up the steps to the hall, but the rain had wet the steps. Slipping, I fell straight into the doorframe.

"Oof!" The entire hall went silent, and everyone turned to look at me.

"Umm…I—" I stammered, blushing under the gaze of so many people.

"Perfect!" The mayor exclaimed before I could get out an apology.

Now, this is a warning to any of you who know a mayor. If they ever look at you amusedly and tell you you're perfect, run! Because the likelihood is they are telling you that you are perfect to go on a mission that could kill you in order to retrieve something you don't believe in.

That's right. He was planning to make me find the talking book I mentioned earlier.

"Well done; we need more young people like you to volunteer," Mayor Clinton said before pausing. "Uh…how old are you, dear?"

"Fourteen," I answered on autopilot.

"Perfect, no one will suspect a young girl. Aren't you a little young for the mission to find the book?" one of the men from the crowd ventured.

"Yes!" I exclaimed, seizing my chance. "You should…um…get someone who actually, well, believes in the book."

That may not have been the smartest thing to say.

"You don't believe?" Grammie asked from her chair. I looked around at the angry, shocked, and scared faces. I almost felt as if I were letting them down by answering.

"I'm sorry; I don't," I finally said. "Maybe Mayor Clinton should choose someone else."

The mayor looked perplexed and fiddled with the short hair on his chin. "No worries," he finally said. "Even better actually."

I choked. "It is?" I almost dreaded hearing the answer.

"Yes." He patted me on the shoulder and turned me to face the crowd. "It is even better because it means she is open minded. She will not be restricted as to where she will go or what she will do. Yes, this is much better."

The faces in the crowd burned hopefully in response. I saw Grammie's face. She no longer looked shocked; instead, her face shone with pride. Her own granddaughter was to embark on such a daring mission. All the rest also stared at me, hope painted on their faces. They were willing to put their faith and trust in me to find this thing.

"It is settled," Clinton said. "Kelly."

"Kayla," I corrected.

"Kayla," he continued, "will go on a journey for the book and will use its last wish to try to help us!"

The crowd lit up and started cheering as I folded in on myself in horror. How could they believe I would just find it? Didn't they realise I didn't know where it was? I didn't even believe in the bloody book, for goodness sake! Where would I even start?

"Do I even get help?" I stuttered, finally willing myself to talk.

There were various scoffs. (Thank you, Mackenzie and Reagon.) But from inside the crowd, I heard a shout.

"I will go with Kayla!" Terry shouted. He walked to the front of the crowd, with Julie in tow.

"And…you?" The mayor asked, looking at Julie behind Terry.

"Well, I guess I'll go too," she said, smiling with an air of feigned distress. "It's probably for the best," she added. "They would have little chance of surviving without at least one person who has sense. Terry knows his way through the woods to Fun City; also, he has been to Fun City with his father. I will just be the brains of the team," Julie said, smiling and flicking her hair up.

The crowd nodded in approval and started cheering, and soon, the cheers rose into a crescendo of "Well done," "Good luck," and "Bravo!"

"Don't worry, Kay," Terry whispered. "We'll do this."

"Don't call me Kay" was my only reply, because I couldn't manage anything else.

I looked around to find Grammie sitting in her chair, with her eyes closed and a very satisfied smile, apparently lost in some old memories.

The cheering had died down, and people were looking at the three of us expectantly. It was as if they expected us to waltz out now and be back in twenty minutes with this book.

"Where do we start?" Julie asked the whole hall in general, breaking through the silence.

It was actually all of the grandparents that answered. They all spoke in unison and gave their answer as if they were telling us Christmas had come early, not as if they wanted to send us to the one place we couldn't go.

"You start at Fun City, of course."

If you started reading this story thinking "Wow, the people of this girl's city are craaaaazy!" you may have been right. Not only are they sending us on this quest for an object I don't even believe in, they want us to start looking for it in Fun City, Atro City's archenemy.

Our grandparents told us that the myth of the book with answers surfaced around the same time they were protesting against pollution. The Council of Unistate decided that it was a ploy to gain more support for the protesters. The myth could have been the tipping point that led the council to round up the protesters and exile them to Atro City.

Many people were looking for the book, when the rumour had surfaced, but no one had found it.

Rumours abounded that there was a map leading to the book. The prime minister had confiscated the map from of one of the protesters before they were exiled, and he had been secretly trying to find out where it led for years.

Now it was our job to find the map and succeed where a prime minister had failed. No pressure.

2029

Later, Terry, Julie, and I ran through the school's corridors in pursuit of our classroom. Being evening time, the corridors were splashed with the red hues of the setting sun. It was strangely quiet, and the sound of our footfalls cut through the eerie silence. We were fetching our daggers and throwing knives, Julie's bow and arrows, and some basic supplies.

"Your phones charged?" Terry asked. We both nodded in response. We strapped on our vests under our shirts, zipped up our cardigans, and secured our knife holders on our arms. We all put on gloves, and Julie and I had to wear leggings made out of tiny chains as it was the fighting kit for girls. They looked like grey leggings but protected us like armour. Once the three of us were ready to go, we headed out of the school premises.

A car had come to pick us up from the school gates. It would take us as close to Fun City's borders as it could. We each hugged our respective parents.

"You'll do great; I know it," my mother said to me.

"Go show the world who's boss," my dad said before hugging me.

Grammie said barely anything; she feared she would cry if she did. Instead, she handed me a strip of paper. It was a bookmark. "It will be important" was all she managed.

"Bye," I said one last time, not 100 percent sure whether I would see them again.

Then I got in the car.

As the driver took off, Terry, Julie, and I sat mostly in silence. The only sounds were the wind and rain as we rushed past, accompanied by the radio, which played the best of Atro City's number-one hits.

I leaned against the window and let the roads blur past me. I watched as Treary Lane passed us by. Then we drove past Droket Avenue, and then the names just ran together, and after that, we drove past fields with the odd power plant or lone farm every so often.

"We'll do this, won't we?" I asked nervously.

Julie patted me on the shoulder. "Yeah, we've had the training, we know each other, and between us, we know how to do it."

I nodded, reassured. That was the great thing about friends—they were always there.

"So once we get there, we should probably use the south entrance," Terry started. "It's the farthest from our city, so people from Fun City probably won't expect us to enter from that side—"

Julie and I grinned at each other. Whenever Terry got into something, he did his research. "And if there are guards?" I interrupted him. He looked at the two of us in turn.

"We'll take them together," he said determinedly.

By this time, we were driving through the remains of the forest near Fun City. Smoking stumps and rotting shrubs were all that remained. The sheer magnitude of the destruction gave only the barest of hints as to how majestic the forest had once been. We saw grey buildings where the trees once would have been. Long and dark, they each supported a crowd of chimneys. Each one let loose its own ribbon of filthy air. Looking above the buildings, I could see where the ribbons all joined into a big foul fog, which was settling down on us.

From some of the tree stumps, wisps of smoke curled into the air. They had just been freshly cut.

As we got closer to Fun City, the number of grey buildings increased, and the number of trees dramatically decreased. Soon, we could make out a faint bronze blur in the distance. We were close to the city's outer walls.

As the car slowed slightly, we saw more and more people milling around the buildings. They wore grey overalls and masks over their mouths. All we could see were their beady eyes as they curiously glanced at us in the car.

"Close the windows," I said. "Look at the fog."

Indeed, as we drove farther forwards, the fog seemed to settle lower and lower. It was as if it could sense my mood getting angrier and angrier as we witnessed more destruction and pollution.

"It's all that pollution," Julie said, referring to the fog. "They just don't care."

"They will when they all die," Terry said grimly. "And I refuse to let it get that bad."

Julie and I looked at him in shock. "You want to help them?" I asked incredulously.

He sighed. "I don't know; not exactly, but if reducing their pollution levels means that we don't pay the price, then I'm willing to consider it."

I sighed. I could see where he was coming from. I didn't want anything to happen to anyone in my family because of the sins of Fun City.

"Don't worry," I said. "We will find this book, and we will be fine."

He also sighed, looking as if he were barely convinced by my words. "But you don't even believe in the book," he countered.

I shrugged. "I could believe in it for now, I guess."

At that point, Julie almost burst into tears. She's a very strange girl at times. "That's so sweet." She sniffed.

I playfully punched her on the arm. "Shut up." I laughed.

Looking outside once more, we saw a small road that veered off to the left from the road we were on. Almost as soon as we had noticed it, the driver suddenly veered onto it. We bumped up and down and rolled over the uneven pebbles and rocks.

We were surrounded on either side by a multitude of grey buildings. The fog that hovered above looked thick and heavy as it was continuously fuelled by the pollutants from the buildings.

Seeing all the fog and tree stumps almost made me sick. How could people do that to their world and not even care? Not only were they harming themselves, but their pollution also had an effect on us. Did that mean nothing? I realised in that moment just how horrible the people of Fun City were. They were willing to put other people's lives at risk just for their fun. It was despicable.

I came out of my thoughts as the three of us hurtled forwards into the back of the front seats. The car skittered to a final halt, and we hit the backs of our own seats. Looking at each other, we unbuckled our belts.

"This is as far as I go," the driver said. We secured our masks, and we got out the car.

We had our mission all planned out. If only it had actually worked. The first few stages of our plan worked. We sneaked around the city in the shade of the grey buildings. We came into sight of the south entrance, just as planned. Then, it went so terribly wrong.

The plan all started going haywire when we ventured out from the shade of the buildings. After the grey buildings stopped, the ground sloped downwards to the gates of the city. It was as if a moat had once run around the city walls. Beyond the line of the grey buildings, the ground was plain and dry, like a barren desert, broken only by the huge city walls. The dry land allowed us to see the wall as it curved around the city. It also, unfortunately, allowed those guarding it to see us.

So it came as no surprise when we were immediately sighted. "Hey, you!" the guards yelled as they saw us.

We broke into a run, foolishly hoping we could outrun them to the large silver gates standing in the bronze wall. They were one of the few things between us and our book.

The first guard tackled me from behind as I ran. I only caught a glimpse of him as I turned and elbowed him squarely in the face. He looked big and burly, and his uniform added to his menacing persona.

A second, shorter guard attacked straight after. In one movement, I ducked, avoiding his punch. As I got back up, I took advantage of his momentum and pulled his leg, thus tripping him up.

From the corner of my eye, I noticed several more guards running towards us, each armed with a gun or knife. Each one looked more menacing and burly than the next. I knew there was no way we could hold off all of them at once.

"We have to outrun them!" I eventually yelled desperately into the remaining two crowds of guards. I knew that Terry and Julie were buried somewhere amongst them. I saw my friends emerge as they pushed the crowds away slightly. Nodding to each other, we ran for it.

I ran as fast as I could, my legs hurting and almost tripping on each step. The ground may have been plain, but it was littered with cracks and pebbles. They served well at tripping us up.

We were quickly nearing the gates now. The tall silver structures stood tall compared to our small sprinting forms. We ran faster still, but we were unable to go straight towards the gates. The guards were chasing us away from that direction, so we had to double back and run alongside the bronze walls. It was either running faster or getting captured.

Up ahead, I finally saw why the guards were chasing us in the direction they were. Some way along the wall, there was a tall arching door. Squinting, I made out the face of yet another man. He was not as burly as the guards and instead wore a suit. He pushed the door open and gestured for us to be brought in.

"They want us to go into that arched door thing," Julie said, panting. She ran over a pebble and tripped slightly, so I had to take her hand and pull her along. More guards were gaining on us now, and we had very few options left as to where to go.

"Well, that's what we are going to have to do," Terry answered grimly. He pulled on my arm, and together, we hurtled through the door and into the unknown.

We blinked to adjust our eyes to the sudden darkness of the room. The door must have opened into a building on the other side of the wall because we didn't walk out into the open city.

The room was long, rectangular, and moderately thin. The left wall was lined with cages, two of which held groups of horrid-looking criminals in green uniforms. Along the right, desks were staggered along the wall. Each one supported its own teetering pile of paper work. Despite the character of the room, we were focused on a door. It innocently stood in the centre of the opposite wall. It was our escape route.

"Come on!" Terry said as we ran. He still had my arm, and I was still dragging Julie, so we all had to run single file through the dark room.

Then Terry tripped.

As far as I could figure, a can had been lying on the floor. Terry slid in multiple directions, dragging us along with him. He went flying and hit the ground, and the rest of us landed on top of him.

"Oof!" The wind was knocked out of me as Julie landed butt first on my stomach (not a fun experience, by the way). For a few moments, we scrambled chaotically, entangled in a pile of our limbs. Eventually, we made it to our feet.

"Let's go," I said. We turned around, only to find the guards had caught up with us. We were surrounded.

I'd like to say we heroically hacked our way through the enemy and made a brave escape, but that wouldn't exactly be the truth.

We did try. We stood back to back and kicked at the guards, but eventually, they took us down.

As I was preoccupied with the two guards in front of me, a third came up behind me and wrapped his arm around me, holding a knife to my neck.

"Stand down, or the girl gets it," he sneered evilly. At that point, Terry and Julie had no choice but to lower their weapons.

Two more guards came behind both Terry and Julie. Within seconds, we all had knives to our throats. Together, the six of us shuffled into one of the cages, and the rest of the guards triumphantly walked out the door at the far end of the room, opposite the one we had come in from.

I looked between Julie and Terry. They were both being forced to stay still in the cage by men who held them. The men were waiting for one of the police men who had left to return with the key to the cage in order to lock it.

"What are you going to do to us?" I spat, disgusted that a Fun City polluter was even touching me.

"We're going to stay like this," the biggest one sneered behind me, "till the boss comes."

"The boss?" Terry asked. "Who's that?" The guard who held him kicked him roughly. Said guard was only a boy, around my age. He had brown hair, and his face was splattered with freckles.

He kicked Terry and said, "None o' your business." Terry winced and tried to rub his inner leg where he had been hit. As I watched him, it gave me an idea, but first, I needed to get that idea over to Julie.

"You people always make the same mistakes," I said suddenly. Julie and Terry both looked at me in confusion. I focused on Julie, looking into her eyes as I talked. I hoped she would get the message.

"You're always so arrogant, for one," I said, and I was kicked in the back of the leg because of it. "And you are always guys." The captors now looked confused, but Julie was slowly starting to grin. She understood what I wanted to do.

"And for another thing, you always stand behind us," I carried on. Julie nodded, and I shouted, "Now!"

Together, Julie and I both kicked backwards and hit our captors between the legs. As my guard doubled over in pain, I turned and elbowed him straight in the head. Julie turned and punched her guard, knocking him out in one fluid motion.

Together, we turned to the third guard, the one who was our age.

"Let him go," I said threateningly, hoping I didn't sound as unsure as I was. After some time, the guard released Terry, and he stumbled over to us. We turned to run out of our prison cell, but the boy blocked the door with his arm.

"Hold up. Where are you going?" he demanded.

"None of your business." Terry spat at him. The boy merely smirked and, looking at the fallen guard, said, "Seeing as you just punched out my uncle, I believe it is." He looked between us with narrowed eyes before finally deciding. "You're Atro City dwellers, aren't you?"

Terry seemed to finally lose his patience and moved forwards to give the boy a piece of his mind, but I held him back. Something about the boy's demeanour wasn't right. His eyes weren't filled with the same kind of hatred that was usually seen in the eyes of people from Fun City who saw people from Atro City for the first time, only curiosity.

"What's it to you?" I said, straining with Terry.

"Because I want to help you," the boy finally said. Terry stilled, and we all stood poised, looking at the stranger.

"Why should we trust you?" Julie demanded. He looked between us again and eventually said, "Because you would be doing something more productive than fighting between yourselves." I let go of Terry, and he stopped straining. "And besides, I know where the map to the book is. That is—I assume—what you are looking for. It was what every other Atro City person who ever came to our City was looking for."

⚞

"Any funny business, and we take him out," Terry whispered to us as we sneaked down the paths of Fun City.

The freckled boy (whose name was Cleo) stopped and gestured to us to hurry up and follow him. The sacred map to the book seemed to be hidden in the most majestic of all the buildings in the city—the prime minister's mansion.

At first, we were all suspicious. It seemed this Cleo fellow was taking us right where we would be easily captured. It seemed, for the meantime, that he had the advantage over us. We had no choice but to follow his word to navigate through this uncharted city of pollution. Although Terry had visited Fun City before, he didn't really know his way around because his visit had been a long time ago and the city had changed. Besides, even if Terry did know his way around the city, Julie and I had no idea where it was we needed to go. So far, Cleo seemed to know both where to go and how to get there, and so we were forced to follow him and trust his word.

We had to lower our mouth masks for the meantime in order to fit in, because we were still trying not to bring attention to ourselves. I tried not to gawk as we passed building after building, each grander than the next. I momentarily let my mind wander away from the pollution as I walked.

The busy streets were lined with a rainforest of buildings. Their tall sides were littered with multitudes of shiny windows, each perfectly aligned and shiny. Squinting against the sun, I made out lone figures on the roofs of the tallest buildings; they paced the lengths of the roofs before lowering themselves over the edges and cleaning the topmost windows.

On the opposite side of the street, the road turned off into an avenue. Each corner was adorned with a glittering hotel. Bright flashing letters proudly stood at the front of each hotel, and below them were fountains that defied the laws of gravity.

Then I looked forwards. Far ahead of us, the street narrowed until it was a walkway. Trees smartly lined the sides of the path, framing the majestic structure that stood behind them. A tall building sat at the end of the path, like the pot at the end of the rainbow. The sun radiated off the polished white marble, making my eyes hurt if I looked at it too long.

We headed down the path, keeping close to the line of trees. The trees seemed to loom threateningly over us, as if they knew we were foreigners. Cleo silently led us up the path until we were at the edge of the royal gardens.

The building seemed to tower over us, but somehow, the domed doors of rustic brown wood looked inviting. At the last second, we veered to the left and went along a small path in the trees.

"This will lead us to the back," Cleo told us. Unlike us, he seemed calm and not at all troubled by the fact that he was leading enemies into home territory. Maybe he did honestly want to help. I was willing to give him a chance. The only problem was that I couldn't figure out why.

We eventually stopped five minutes later at the back of the building. From the back, it didn't look nearly as inviting. Pipes ran out the back of the building like veins attached to a lone annex behind. The annex was letting off huge amounts of steam and smoke, shuddering with the work. At the back of the prime minister's mansion was a small grey door chained shut on one side to the wall. Apart from that, the place looked empty, which put me on guard.

"Why is there no one here?" Julianna asked, seemingly reading my mind. She too looked troubled and tired.

"They don't expect people to get this far; they usually catch people before they get this far into the city," Cleo replied, looking up at the sky.

"But shouldn't they be on guard because we escaped here?" I asked, thinking about how easily we had got here.

"Well, according to everyone else, you are still locked up in prison," he said, taking notice of our shocked faces. "What? You didn't think I would sell you out, did you?"

"Yes," I said bluntly. "Yes, we did."

We stopped to eat sandwiches we had brought from the corner shop Cleo had recommended, secured our mouth masks, and found a rock.

Then, we threw the rock at the chains. These Fun City guys must have been really sure no one would make it this far because the lock crumbled like a cookie. (A normal cookie mind you, not one of Julie's homemade things. Just a warning: they *will* break your teeth.)

When we were about to sneak through the door, Terry made us wait. It turned out he had drunk a little too much water with lunch. After a few minutes whilst Julie, Cleo, and I waited awkwardly, we finally made it inside.

Even though we were in the back of the prime minister's mansion, it was still far more resplendent than anything I had ever had the honour of stepping foot in before or even seen. The walls were lined with portraits, visually telling the history of who had ruled Fun City.

As we neared the front of the majestic building, there were podiums telling the history of the city. Closer to the front doors, we began to notice red carpets that blanketed the floors and were edged by purple ropes, which drew us along a certain path.

"Why are you leading us towards the front?" Terry asked uncomfortably. We did *not* need another friendly meeting with the guards. I was starting to become doubtful; what if Cleo planned to turn us in?

"I'm not turning you in," Cleo said, as if reading our minds. He scowled slightly at our lack of trust, and his freckles gathered near his eyes. "It's just that the prime minister's office is on the third floor, and the stairs are just at the next turn," he finished.

The rest of us looked at each other in horror. "The map is in the prime minister's *office*!" Julie said, turning pale. "Well, this just got a little more impossible."

There were tour groups being led through the large domed doors when we peeked around the corner. We would have to cause a distraction or hope they didn't see us. We looked around the corner once more, and I had to hold on to the hood of my jumper as the breeze from the open doors cut through the warmth inside.

"Look." I said as I watched a group of tourists who were gathered by the front doors. "The tour group is leaving the entrance hallway." And they were. Only now, they were coming straight towards us.

"Quick." Terry stumbled backwards and pulled us along with him. "Back the other way."

"But it will take longer," Cleo complained, running along with us anyway.

"Well, too bad," I replied, pulling Cleo along by the arm to make sure he wouldn't start running in the opposite direction. I didn't trust him not to get us arrested *yet*.

We ran back the other way. I recognised the pictures from when we had passed through the first time. We got to a crossroad, where we had the option to carry on into foreign corridors or go back outside. We heard the footsteps and curious voices of the tourists as they approached.

"We'll have to go back outside," Cleo told us. But I had other ideas. I had noticed a fire-escape ladder right next to the window. It would be better to climb up it to the third floor than go outside because if Terry, Julie, Cleo, and I went outside, we would have to sneak back in and to the front of the mansion to get to the stairs. At least if we used the fire escape, we could get to the third floor without having to worry about tourists.

"We *won't* go outside," I said through clenched teeth as I dragged Terry over to the window. Together, we strained with it, willing it to open.

"Hurry," Cleo hissed. "Let's just go outside." The footsteps were louder now, and Terry and I had almost gotten the window latch open.

"Hurry," I said as we pulled. The footsteps had almost caught up with us.

"Uh…yes!" Terry said as we finally undid the latch and pushed the window wide open.

"Quickly," I said as I shuffled Julie through the window. She put her foot on the ledge and jumped up, securing a hold on the ladder. She climbed up, and Cleo and I followed; I went first and then helped Cleo up.

"Quickly. Climb!" I said as I held my hand down for Terry. I could hear the voices clearly now. We could not get caught. Terry put his foot on the ledge, and I hung as low as I could, but then the tour group came around the corner.

"Uh!" Terry exclaimed as he dived under the window ledge and onto the grass.

"What was that then?" I heard one of the tourists ask. Julie and Cleo pulled me up some, so I wasn't hanging over the window. We hung there, awkwardly and silently, as an old lady poked her head out the window.

I could hardly breathe as I tried not to move. I willed my hair not to sway in the breeze and Julie and Cleo not to drop me.

After what seemed like an age, the woman's head retreated back into the hallway, and we heard the buzz of conversation as the tour group walked off. I sighed in relief, and my breathing returned to normal.

"Quick," I whispered to Terry. I could feel the blood rushing to my head as I hung upside down. Eventually, our hands clasped, and he climbed up my arm and onto the ladder above me. Terry and Julie both pulled me the right way around, and we started to climb up the ladder.

As we climbed, we had to navigate around the mass of pipes that ran out the back of the building and into the annex. At one point, I almost lost my footing and ended up hanging from one of the pipes. I then made the mistake of looking down. I realised the hard way just how high up the prime minister's office must be.

Finally, we approached a windowsill. Cleo pushed Julie's feet up so she could climb through, and from there, she helped all of us up.

We had made it.

All around us was pure glory. The prime minister's office was something to be proud of. The door was opposite the window, and on either side of it sat glass cabinets that brimmed with trophies and shields.

With its back to the window sat a desk. It was overflowing with paper work, but even under all of that, I could tell the wooden desk had been craft-ed from the best kind of wood and by the best kind of people.

Each corner of the room was adorned with a flag, the flag of Fun City. Its motto was engraved on the wall, which was basically a sentence full of sheer boastfulness.

"I'll go out and stand guard," Terry said. He knew he was perfectly rub-bish at all the patient-looking stuff. He could spend hours planning and re-searching *before* a mission, but once he got *on* one, he was all action.

As he exited the room, Julie, Cleo, and I ransacked the room. The first place we checked was the desk. We looked in all the drawers, but the only things we found were boring papers and a postcard with a dog in an Easter bunny costume on it.

We went through pretty much every paper on the desk, but it turned out they were just papers to be signed. We did find one interesting letter—the reply to the complaint letter the mayor of Atro City had sent. It had obviously been forgotten about because I knew the mayor wrote that letter months ago. Julie pocketed it to give to the mayor once we got back home.

We had spent about three hours looking through the room, and so far, we had found nothing.

"It's here. My dad told me so!" Cleo stated. His brown hair flopped around his head as he bounced around the room in search of the map.

Julie was pacing on the thin red carpet by the door. I found it odd how the carpet only covered one small strip of the room by the door, but I didn't complain. I suppose people had their own tastes. However, I did eventually have to tell Julie to stop pacing.

"You'll wear a hole in the carpet," I warned.

She waved me away with her hand and said, "Don't worry, Kayla. It's not that thin a carpet." So of course, she wore a hole in the carpet.

"Julie, now they are going to know we were here," I hissed. We bent down and tried to adjust the carpet so no one would see the hole. We tried to turn the carpet so the flagpole covered the hole, but when we hammered it into the skirting, it wouldn't stay.

I tucked the carpet and tried again. Bang, bang, bang, thud. I stopped and banged again. Sure enough, I heard a thud as I pounded on a certain part of the carpet.

"Julie," I called. "Help me pull the floorboard up; I think it's hollow underneath."

Julie and Cleo rushed over, and together, we pulled on the floorboard. Slowly, it flipped over as if it were on hinges. Once it had rotated 180 degrees, we saw what was underneath. Glued to the floorboard was a box. It was golden and had a small clasp on the front. The top had a small sticker on it that read "Important. Atro City fuel."

"This is it," Julie said. "I know it."

Excited, we started to pull the box open only to find it was locked. I took the bookmark Grammie had given me and folded it. Then we tried to pick the lock with the hard corner. We were so engrossed with opening the box, we didn't hear the shouts until they were just around the corner.

"Trespassers, we know you are there. Show yourselves," I heard guards voices shouting from somewhere in the corridor.

Julie, Cleo, and I looked at each other in horror. "Guards," I eventually said, and we started pulling desperately at the box.

Terry ran through the door, out of breath and with a cut on his cheek. "I couldn't stop them," he said. "We don't have much time."

I gestured to him to come and help us, and I got up to go and take on the guards. Terry took hold of my arm. "Be careful," he said. "I know you've trained in hand-to-hand combat, but they are brutal."

I smiled grimly. "I'll use one of my weird ideas."

I slipped the bookmark into Terry's hands; I had a feeling I needed to keep it safe, and keeping it with me whilst fighting the guards wouldn't be the safest idea. "Make sure it stays safe," I told him. Then I turned and barrelled out the door.

"Over here," I yelled, waving my arms. The guards turned and followed me, and I ran in the opposite direction. I heard them following me and had to duck as I heard a gunshot.

I turned left, then right, and then took a few more turns until finally, I was running down a new corridor, which had doors lining both sides. I heard half of the guards run straight past the turning, but some followed me around. I carried on running, stopping only to punch one of the closest guards.

At the last minute, I ducked into one of the doors on the right. I stood behind the door, ready to attack, but the rest of the guards ran past the door.

With a sigh of relief, I turned, only to stop in surprise. The room was only the size of a closet, but everywhere I looked there were large metal cylinders, each filled with fuel.

"Jet fuel...car fuel," I read as I walked around the room. I approached the back, where there was a lone set of shelves right in the middle. A set of dark curtains billowed around its frame. I realised there must be a window behind the shelves. Maybe I could push the shelves out of the way, and we could try to escape out of the window. There was no way we could go downstairs now; the guards would probably shoot us on sight.

Placing my hands on the sides of the shelves, I pushed, placing all of my weight in my arms. The structure teetered from the top, and I sort of managed to wobble it over enough so I could slide past it and to the window.

Carefully, I undid the latch on the window, and it flew open. The smelly fog blew in, and I looked outside. Below, I could see the pipes coming out of the building, so I must have doubled back at some point. The annex looked small and scary against the rapidly darkening sky.

"Kayla!" I turned, my knife out, ready to slice up the attacker, but it was only Julie.

"Julie," I said as she checked me over for cuts. I had only one on my arm, which I must have gotten whilst running.

"I managed to free the window; we can climb down this way."

She looked past me, making a small face at the fog, but nodded. "We got the box," she said. This time, I looked past her to Terry, who grinned slightly as he turned, showing me the floorboard protruding out of his backpack.

"The glue was too strong, so we took the whole board," he said, handing me it. "Here, you look."

I took it but didn't look at it. Instead, I pointed him and Cleo to the window.

"I got us an escape," I said.

Then we heard a gruff, triumphant voice from the doorway. "Too bad it won't work."

1967

It had been a long ride to the Main Hall of Unistate, but Lily's mind had been racing the whole time. She had tried to convince her parents against going to the meeting (her family had also been invited), but it had all been in vain. They wanted to go, and she couldn't convince them otherwise.

She shook with nerves every time she considered what could happen. The prime minister could find out she was one of the Ecos. He could force her to reveal her friends' identities. She could slip up and give the whole game away. In some ways, she wished she didn't have to go at all.

"You shouldn't," Tyler had said to her. "The letter says it wants you to come. Not that you have to." Although Lily agreed with him, she couldn't refuse the invitation. It would only make her seem more suspicious.

Tyler Stevenson was Lily's boyfriend. He was one of the only people who knew the Ecos but wasn't in the group. The only other person was Jacob's brother, but they trusted him with the secret.

Tyler had been adamantly against Lily going to the meeting. He feared for her safety almost more than she did. He hadn't wanted her to go, but she had insisted she did. He had known better than to argue with her. She was very stubborn when she wanted to be.

She sighed for the umpteenth time.

"You'll be fine," her dad assured her from the front seat of the car. She sighed. Her parents had taken her nervousness to be fear of policemen. If only they knew.

"You're right," Lily sighed, though the faint stirring of uneasiness remained. What if something did go wrong?

There was no time left for her pondering as the car wheeled to a stop. In front of them stood the grand structure that was the Main Hall. It was completely round in shape, the bricks having been carved with cylindrical designs to add to the effect. Round stairs twisted and turned, leading to the main door. Lily thought it looked like a giant, grey bee hive.

Hesitating slightly, she got out of the car. The wind hit her hard in the face, blowing her dark hair around her. Head bent against the wind, she followed her parents into the hall.

The room was just as grand on the inside as it was on the outside. Tables leaned against the walls the whole way around the room. At each table sat a family being interrogated by equally horrid-looking men in uniform.

Lily had to smile when she saw her friend Willow interrogating a rather friendly looking family. Willow was interrogating them to find the Ecos members' identities when secretly she was one herself.

Willow Daniels was probably the oldest in the group. Twenty-three years of age, she worked closely with Unistate's police force. She had been employed to interrogate the families, and so she was able to keep her ear to the ground in case anyone slipped up and revealed something. If they did, she would then be prepared to make up a story that would pass off the slip up.

With a start, Lily realised she had once again been engrossed in her thoughts. A tug on her arm told her that her family was about to be interrogated. Following her parents, Lily wove through the waiting families and sat at a table at the back of the room.

The table was littered with yellow folders, each printed with the name of a citizen of Unistate. Behind the desk sat a tired-looking man. He had dirty-blond hair that fell carelessly on his head and dark eyes that burned with boredom. It was obvious he would rather have been anywhere else than where he was.

"Name?" he asked in a monotone.

"Susan Mandy," her mother said. The man rifled through the piles until he found one with Susan's name on it. He looked expectantly at Lily's father.

"James Mandy," he answered. The man searched once again until he found James's file. He then looked at Lily.

"Lily Mandy," she also replied, watching as he found her own record. She briefly wondered what was written in there. What did they know about her? With a mental smile of satisfaction, she realised that the one thing that could be useful to the policemen's investigation, they didn't know. She was hoping she could keep it that way.

"So," the man said, looking at Susan's file. "You were born on the twenty-fourth of April, 1923." He looked up at Lily's mother. "Is that right?"

She nodded. "It is."

The man nodded and ticked something off in Susan's file. Then he asked her to describe her weekly routine.

He asked the same questions of Lily's dad. He confirmed his birth details and then gave a detailed account of what he did every week. Then it was Lily's turn.

"Born on July twenty-ninth, 1950?" the man asked, looking at her. She nodded.

"So that makes you seventeen," he murmured, writing in her file. He looked back up at her. "What do you do every week?" he asked.

Lily could have sworn he was looking far more interested in *her* routine than he had in her parents but wasn't sure if this was just her opinion or not.

"Well, Monday to Friday, I attend the local secondary school," she started. He held up a hand.

"No after-school clubs or outside-of-school activities on those days?" he asked.

"No." She sighed. "I don't attend any clubs on weekdays." He wrote in her file again.

"So your parents see you at every other time of the day when you're not at school?" he checked.

She sighed once again. The questions hadn't been so thorough for her parents.

"No," she answered patiently. "I walk home with my friends—"

ANI TALWAR

"Who are your friends?" he interrupted. On her lap, Lily's hands fisted. If the man was going to interrogate her so thoroughly, the least he could do was be nice about it.

"I walk with my friends Tyler Stevenson and Willow Daniels and—"

"Why do you walk and not just drive?" The man interrupted her again.

"Because my mother and father don't finish work in time to pick me up," she said between clenched teeth. It was a struggle to keep the annoyance out of her voice. "They get home just before I do when I walk," Lily finished.

The man narrowed his eyes at her, and she pushed down a sigh of irritation. "Is that all you do?" he asked suspiciously.

"Yes," she managed.

"You don't participate in any *secret* activities, say, campaigning against pollution?" he asked, staring directly at Lily.

She locked eyes with him, silently daring him to challenge her answer. This man had decided that Lily was one of the Ecos, and whilst he was right, she wasn't about to give him the satisfaction of knowing so.

"No," she answered finally. "Walking is *all* I do."

He leafed through the pages of her file, apparently defeated. She allowed herself a quick smile of satisfaction. Getting information out of her wasn't going to be as easy as he might have thought.

However, her interrogation was apparently not over yet. The man, now inspired to change his tone by the fact that he had apparently failed to prove Lily was an Eco, looked up at her.

"What do you do on weekends?"

She sighed. If he had gotten that suspicious about her weekday routine, what would he say about her weekend routine? Especially when her Ecos meetings were on weekends.

"Homework," she replied wearily. No point mentioning a weekly club if she didn't have to.

"What homework?" he said, narrowing his eyes.

"Whatever homework I'm set!" she exclaimed. Of all the things to ask her! The interrogator's mouth curled into a soft smile. He was obviously happy to have provoked her into saying something more than calm phrases. She

mentally made a note to calm down. She couldn't get angry and let it slip that she was one of the Ecos.

"Any clubs?" he asked her, staring directly into her eyes for any sign of hesitation.

It's not a club, it's a group project, she thought. "No," she answered. He leaned forwards, looking intently at her.

"Are you sure? No *secret* club?" he persisted.

She forced herself to meet his gaze. She didn't want him to get *any* inkling of her real routine. Besides, she thought, it's not exactly secret if we make our club's aims public.

"No," she finally answered. "No *secret* clubs."

He narrowed his eyes. She could see the fierce fire of determination burning in the whites of his eyes. He was hell bent on proving her to be an Eco.

"Are you sure that's your answer?" he asked smoothly. "Because you know what will happen if you lie."

She didn't trust herself to speak. She didn't want to give anything away. Instead, she shook her head. A smug smile touched his lips as he continued.

"I'm sure you've heard of the derelict village not far from us. The one that was killed off by famine and plague. That's where we send the liars. The ones who are doing this campaign. The ones who are disrupting the peace in our home."

Lily's mind was racing. If she didn't lie, was that really the fate that would befall her? She considered telling him. Maybe they would let her off, and she would be able to live happily if she apologised.

"Should I tell…" she muttered unconsciously to herself, unaware of the interrogator as he leaned in to hear what she had said.

"Tell us what?" he asked slyly, dark eyes glistening with triumph. With a start, she realised she must have spoken aloud.

"N-nothing!" she stammered, but she knew the shocked look on her face had given her away. He had caught her, and she had fallen right into his trap.

"Now, missy," he said, rising to his feet triumphantly. Through her hammering heartbeat, Lily heard her parents gasp in shock as they also realised the truth.

The man carried on with barely concealed happiness. "Let us take you away to…" He stopped. Lily broke away from her horror long enough to see what he was looking at. He was staring over her shoulder in some sort of shock. Turning around, she saw why.

Around twenty uniformed policemen had entered the room and were surrounding a boy who stood defiantly despite being held by both arms.

"Success," one of the policemen said, raising the boy's arm for everyone to see. "We have caught an Eco," he stated.

At once, all the officers were on their feet and approaching the boy. Through the crowd of people, Lily could only make out the mop of coloured hair, but that was enough. She knew who it was instantly—Trevor Davies, the prime minister's nephew.

Lily shook with fear. More than one Eco had been caught. Their plans were falling apart. Behind her, she could sense the man who had questioned her looking closely at her. He was the only one who hadn't hurried off at the sight of the boy. She knew why that was. It was so he could make sure she couldn't escape.

Suddenly, she heard a shout. Looking back at the crowd, she noticed Trevor. He had broken out of the officers' grip and had somehow gotten a gun.

"Get down, or I'll shoot!" he shouted. A few of the closer officers dropped to the floor, but Lily could hear the fear in Trevor's voice. As the officers ducked, Trevor's eyes flicked in her direction. His eyes widened, and then he discretely flicked his eyes towards the door. She understood his message. He wanted her to run whilst she could.

Once more, he pointed the gun in her general direction. He waited and then shot. Instantly, everyone but Lily was down on the floor. He nodded to her again.

She hated his plan; she didn't want to let him get arrested and exiled. However, she knew that if she didn't run, they would both end up in trouble. So, hating it all the more, she took advantage of the chaos and ran.

2029

We whirled around, weapons at the ready, only to sag in dismay. It seemed the guards had all found each other and then us.

"Try us," Terry said. He stepped out in front of me to take the attention off the board in my hand. "You will only live to regret trying to stop us," he added, but I could hear the fear in his voice.

The guards scrutinised us. Julie's hair was in tangles, and her face was tired. Cleo, one of their own, had led enemies into home territory. Terry was glaring hatefully, and the cut on his cheek was bleeding, and I had a floorboard in my hand.

"Well, we can see about that." The guard on the left sneered. Then they charged.

I saw Cleo, Terry, and Julie defending about three guards each, but five guards came at me. Four of them had daggers—the fifth, a gun.

I swung the floorboard, thwacking each one in the face in turn. I turned to the closest one and punched him. Two of the others tried to attack again. One of them slashed at me with his dagger. I ducked out the way and pulled out my own dagger, using the hard handle to knock him out.

The other stabbed, but I leaned to the side, wincing as he managed to graze my side. I pulled his stabbing arm farther forwards, and he went face first into a metal fuel tank.

I was so engrossed in taking down the other four guards that I didn't notice the fifth one with the gun until Terry shouted.

"Don't shoot, you moron! You'll blow us all up."

It was then that I took a look over at the guard. He had a wild amount of piercings all over his face and a cruel grin as he aimed his gun at a fuel tank. The other guards had either woken up or forgotten about us, and they too were looking at the gunman, who ignored them. He really was going to blow us up.

"RUN!" Terry yelled, and we made for the nearest exit which happened to be the window.

It all seemed to happen in slow motion. The four of us ran straight for the window. Fear lit up all our faces, and urgency sped our moves.

We all leaped, in what seemed like unison, straight for the windowsill, but before we could land on it, we were all propelled forwards. I felt the heat of the explosion on my back as I hurtled through the window, wincing as I felt broken wood scrape my legs.

For a few seconds, I managed to focus; I saw the ground coming towards me, but there was something else—one of the pipes. My free arm flailed out in front of me, desperately trying to grasp anything that would stop me from becoming a Kayla pancake.

However, it was my leg that caught the pipe. My foot hooked onto it, and my momentum caused me to swing around and around the pipe, hanging by only my legs. Through the swirl and blurriness, I made out the figure of Terry: his face was a picture of terror as he tried to grab on to anything.

"Terry!" I shouted desperately, still spinning but with one arm out. I felt his hand grab on to mine and clasp tightly, and I sighed in relief. Then his weight pulled us down.

I swung down in one fluid arc, curling my legs around the pole in a hope of not falling. Together, we slowed to a stop. I looked down at Terry's face, which was looking up at me with relief.

"Thanks, Kay," he panted.

"No problem, but don't call me Kay," I said, trying not to slur my words because I was upside down.

We hung silently, and I looked around. Through the building's window, I could see the fire close to its frame. It had only been a small explosion from one tank, but if the fire spread to the others, it could cause a lot more damage.

I looked around for Cleo and Julie. Julie was lying unconscious on the grass below, against the annex. I had a bad feeling she would get arrested if found there.

"Take it," Terry said suddenly to me.

"Take what?" I asked, confused. He nodded to our linked hands, and I realised there was something between them. It was cold and thin. "The bookmark!" I said.

He nodded up at me and repeated, "Take it."

I was confused. "Why?"

"Because I don't want to be held responsible for losing it," he said, looking down at Julie.

"Then put it in your pocket or something. You can give it to me later," I said.

He looked up at me. "Take it," he repeated a third time. "In case I'm not there to give it to you."

I was getting worried now. "What are you on about, Terry?" I asked him forcefully.

He looked up at the fire, which had almost touched the other fuel tanks now.

"That thing's going to explode," he said. "And we're all going to go in different directions into the forest." I looked behind the annex at the forest. It started at one corner of the prime minister's mansion, curved around the back of the annex, and touched the other back corner of the house. Even from as high as I was, I couldn't see the end.

"Well, I will just keep hold of you," I said, hoping I would be able to.

He smiled sadly, as if I had said something funny. "See you, Kay," he said.

"Don't call me Kay," I muttered reflexively, somewhat confused.

Then the top floor exploded.

I couldn't hold on with my legs this time. Rubble and bricks were flying past me, and I was pushed by the force. I looked down at Julie's fallen form, but there was nothing I could do. I was spinning, heading straight for the trees.

My hand was wrapped tightly around Terry's. I refused to let him go. However, fiery debris was flying past us, like comets. The pieces were spinning, with their sharp edges glinting dangerously.

"Let go!" Terry said as a sharp, ignited piece of rubble soared towards us. I didn't want to let go; I refused to let Terry be right. He started struggling, and in the end, I had to let go. It was that or he would lose his arm.

"Terry!" I called after him as he was hit by rubble and pushed in another direction. I too was changing direction. I was now going down.

"Ah!" was the only thing I could say as I was dumped into a treetop and left to fall to the hard ground below.

I hit the ground hard, and the wind was knocked out of me. I could barely move. My arm was sending pain waves up my body, where my previous cut had been pulled farther open, and dirt had gotten in.

I could see the green of the tree above me, and imagined the stars, casually splashed on the dark-blue sky above. It was so still and quiet; I could only hear the sounds of the fire, flickering from the house. I could no longer tell where the house was anymore. I could no longer tell where *I* was.

Maybe I'll just sleep for a bit, I murmured to myself, and I fell into a much-needed doze.

The next morning, my stomach woke me. It was being rather rude and thought its emptiness was more important than my sleep.

I pushed myself up slowly, taking in my surroundings for the first time. I realised I had landed deep in the forest. I could not hear any noises, so the house must have been far away. The trees towered over me, their limbs lushly green and speckled with fruit.

My backpack had fallen a few feet to my right, but I could not see the floorboard. I stood up quickly. I needed that floorboard. I ran around the small area, looking everywhere and muttering to myself as I looked. Don't... can't lose it...most important...Julie said.

I stopped. Julie!

I didn't know what had happened to her or where Terry had landed. I hadn't even seen Cleo at all through the explosion.

Finally! I sighed as I found what was left of the floorboard. It had landed harshly on a bolder, and the box had been reduced to splinters. I reached into the pile and pulled out the papers. I flicked through them for a moment before depositing them in my backpack.

Upon opening the backpack, I had to take out the water bottles and my little lunchbox, all of which had cracked and leaked out their contents during the fall. So now, I had no food and no drink, but I did still have a dagger, one bandage, some stray plasters, my bookmark, and my phone, which had been inside a fluffy sock, which was in a box.

I turned it on and noticed I had two messages.

"How are you, darling? Call us soon. Mum and Dad."

"Did you have anything to do with this honey? Dad."

The picture attached with the message was of the prime minister's mansion in flames, and I could make out myself in the corner, hanging from a pipe with Terry holding on to me.

I replied, "Yes. Like my work? It wasn't my fault. I'm OK. Don't know where anyone else is yet. TTYL. Kayla."

I tried calling Terry and Julie, but neither of them picked up. Sighing, I put my phone back in its sock and checked myself for injuries. I had one cut on my arm that desperately needed cleaning and one on my leg, right by the ankle. I managed to use some salvaged water from the shreds of a water bottle to clean the cut on my arm and bandage it, but I had nothing to put on my leg. I placed all my stuff back in my backpack and started looking around.

I didn't know where I was walking to or where I needed to go, but I just walked, hoping that I would find someone. I watched the sky, almost as if it would lead me to where I needed to go. I was starving and feeling more lost by the minute.

Just when I had almost decided to stop and just sit, I heard a voice. It was only faint, but it sounded urgent and scared. It sounded like Julie, or was it Terry? No, it was Julie, or was it? My brain couldn't decide; it was too tired. After deciding it must be both of them shouting together, I ran.

"Kayla!" they shouted again. I turned and ran in the other direction. I heard them again from behind me and whirled around. Then I heard them a third time, from behind me again. I turned once more and sprinted as fast as

I could, only to skid to a halt a few minutes later. I had reached the mansion again. I ran back to hide in the shade as I took in the sight.

Builders littered the area, working at rebuilding the top of the house. They didn't seem to be working hard. They were loitering and laughing gruffly. There were portable toilets in a line near me and even showers! I longed to use one of them, but I had noticed more useful things. Near the trees, there was a table that the builders were obviously using, as it was piled high with ropes and hooks on one side and platefuls of sandwiches, bottles of water, and napkins on the other side.

My eyes lit up. There was food! Real-life food, and water too! I almost started to run and get a sandwich, but I didn't want to steal. I crept closer to the edge of the trees, debating whether or not to take a sandwich, when I heard one of the builders say, "Mmm, those sandwiches hit the spot. Shame they gave us way too many. Everyone's full, and there are still so many left!"

I grinned. If the builders didn't want the sandwiches, then it was OK if I took one.

I sneaked around towards the table, staying in the trees, and noticed a tree branch that hung over it. I grinned as an idea formed in my head.

"Now," I muttered, "that is a plan."

Ten minutes later, I was sitting on the branch, with my hoodie providing a soft layer between my knee and the tree, looking hungrily down at the platter of food and equipment. In one fluid movement, I leaned backwards and was, for the third time in two days, hanging upside down.

First, I picked up a piece of rope that was torn and had a note on it saying it should be thrown away. I also took several bottles of water from a cooler on the table that hadn't been touched because of an Out of Order sign. I had heard some of the builders saying they were just going to throw that water away. I also took a large wad of napkins to help wrap up wounds and so forth.

Then, after pulling myself to a sitting position, I had my fill of a good five sandwiches that I had picked up, before swinging to get over a dozen more sandwiches and wrapping them in napkins for the others when I found them. I *would* find them. After eating and downing one of the bottles of water, I climbed up higher into the tree and perched comfortably on a branch where I had full view of pretty much everything nearby.

For a few minutes, I was content to just watch the builders and the scene below. The annex had been completely blown to smithereens, and where the pile of remains stood, so did a makeshift police cage with a small girl in it.

I watched the girl as she woke up and realised where she was. Her scared face looked around warily, and her blond hair bobbed as she took in her surroundings. I felt sort of sorry for her. She looked a lot like Julie actually. I sat there, staring down and contemplating that thought. Then the girl looked up. She looked straight at me, and I almost fell out of the tree in shock. For the girl sitting there was actually Julie!

I scampered down the tree, leaping silently into the mud at the bottom. I sneaked in the shade until I had a good view of her. Waiting till the builders had mostly turned the other way, I rushed over to her.

"Julie! Oh no, are you hurt?" I whispered as I held on to the bars on her cage. The door was chained shut, but it was not chained tightly, so the door was ajar, but only by a few inches.

"I'm fine," she said, noticing my eye on the small gap. "But there is no way I can fit through there."

I sighed as I examined the cage. There was a large padlock on the chains that kept the door shut. If only I could find the key. But there was no key; I would have to come up with one of my weird ideas.

"Kayla…" Julie said.

"Hang on." I reprimanded her, busy scrutinising the chains. Maybe I could do a Houdini sort of thing to the chains. I had read about it in a magic book in the library.

"Kayla!" she repeated, with more force this time.

"Wait!" I said, toying with the idea of using a hairpin to free her.

"Kayla, run!" Julie yelled again, and this time, I looked up to see what she was yelling about.

Crowded around on all sides stood the builders. Their work suits made them look stocky and menacing as they towered around me. I slowly rose to my feet, turning to face them and silently slipping a dagger through the bars of the cage to Julie.

How would I get out of this one? At once, one of my weird ideas flew into my head.

"Blue eagle!" I shouted, pointing behind them. The builders must have been really stupid because they actually trusted me and looked back.

"I'll be back!" I shouted as I ran straight past the builders, around the side of the mansion, and towards the rest of the city.

I could hear the footfalls of the crowd as they ran after me. "Get her!" I heard and rolled my eyes. As if it wasn't obvious they were trying to catch me. I broke through the trees into the main city area. Buildings were lit up with big screens showing the live chase after the criminal girl. I saw my face magnified and tried to hide behind my hood. I curved around another building and into an alleyway, where I skidded to a halt.

It was a dead end. I scanned the buildings, each of which rose high, sandwiching me into a small dark space. I dashed towards a rickety fire-escape ladder running up the wall, hoping the builders wouldn't see me.

The ladder careened backwards due to my weight as I climbed higher and higher, and I could actually touch the wall of the building on the other side of the alley way as the ladder swayed away from the wall it was attached to. Pushing the wall on the opposite side of the alley slightly with my hand, I sent the ladder back towards the building it was meant to be attached to. Deciding I wasn't going die because of this ladder, I clambered onto the nearest windowsill and fell into the room below.

The window was one of those thin slat types that are high up the walls of tall rooms. I dropped down hard, crashed into an easel, and got a whole lot of paint on my rear end. It was just my luck that it was brown paint.

Stumbling to my feet, I dashed out the room and into a corridor. Paintings lined bright-red walls, which should not have been matched with the bright-orange carpet on the floor. I ran, making numerous turns, until I found a dead end. I turned to find a builder behind me. He smirked.

"They didn't believe me when I said I saw you in here," he said. "But they will when I bring you to them."

"That's if you can," I said, kicking him in the stomach. He returned a punch that sent me reeling back. My cheekbone felt as if it were getting heavier and trying to drop out of my face. He pulled a knife out of his belt, and I copied his move.

He started off by trying to cut my arm, but I defended and made a swipe at his leg. He drew back, and I saw the light shine on something hanging off his belt. It was a small key. I slashed forwards as if I were going to cut his leg, but I changed direction at the last minute and broke the chain on his belt. Grabbing the key, I ran.

I had no idea where I was going, and my legs hurt now as I ran. I finally found a staircase and literally fell down them till I reached the bottom floor. Glimpsing the main doors ahead, I ran out of the building.

The cold, smelly fog hit me hard in the face, making my eyes sting and my ears hurt. Turning around, I saw the glittering sign for Orange's Hotel. I paused outside the doors, looking for the glowing white walls of the prime minister's mansion. Finding it, I ran blindly in that direction.

I don't know how long I ran, but it felt like hours. Finally, I reached the back of the building. I knew Julie was around the corner.

I surged around the corner only to halt in dismay. It seemed the builders weren't as slack as last time. Two had remained, and they sneered proudly as they laid their beady eyes on me.

"Lookee what the cat dragged in," the one on the left drawled smugly. He wore an orange oversuit and a multitude of rings and necklaces, which made him look as if he would be better suited as a rock star, not a builder.

"Goody," the second, shier one added. "Now we will get the post."

I turned to Julie, half afraid to ask.

"The post?"

They grinned triumphantly, glad that they had one over the girl that had repeatedly outsmarted them.

"The post," the ringed one repeated. "You see, lassie, the one who catches the girl who managed to turn our very own boy into a traitor gets the post—the reward, the right to condemn him."

He stepped forwards eagerly. "Stay with 'er," he said to the shier one before running past me and around the corner, ready to boast about his good catch.

I was left alone with the timid guard; he looked resolutely ahead, only glancing guiltily back at me from time to time.

"You can let me go," I said, trying to tempt his guilt. "I could say I fought you off; no one would ever know."

He looked in the direction the first builder had gone in. "No, you wouldn't," he said after a time, finally gathering up his courage. "You wouldn't tell them a thing; you would just run and let me get arrested." He paced, his anger fully fuelled now. "No. I will not let you go," he said. "In fact..."

Picking a rope up from the table, he roughly pushed me at the cage. Wrapping the rope around my wrists, he slipped the other end through the gap and tied it to both of Julie's wrists.

"Try outsmarting that," he said, turning back to guarding us.

I tugged at the rope, hoping there was a weak spot, but there was none.

I sat, dejected. How had I let this happen? The whole time, I had been so careful. I hadn't fought with the builders but ran, I thought, well, except for that one builder in that orange hotel. But that was only because he had the...

"The key!" I whispered excitedly. Julie looked up at me, confused.

"What key?" she replied.

Straining to reach my pocket, I retrieved the small silver object. "The key to get you out of there, of course," I replied. I handed her the key awkwardly because of the rope, and she undid the lock and dropped the chains to the ground whilst I guarded her.

"Move back so I can open the gate," Julie whispered. She opened the gate, sending me into panic once when it squeaked. Finally, we got the gate open, and slowly, we sneaked into the forest that had fast become our ally.

"Hey!" We heard a shout behind us, followed by a gunshot. Julie and I hit the floor, neither of us wanting to be blown to bits. After some time, we stood up to continue running, but more gunshots followed us, and we wouldn't run fast because our wrists were still tied together.

"Ah!" My foot rolled sideways, and I fell to the floor, almost dragging Julie down with me. She pulled me to my feet.

"Come on!" she said between clenched teeth as she pulled me up. She ran, and I hopped slightly behind her. Three more gunshots followed us as we dodged between trees.

"We're going to become the world's first human sushi if this keeps up," Julie panted finally. She pulled me to a tree, ducking as we heard more shots.

"Are you mad?" I asked. Julie was climbing the tree!

"We will die if we keep this up; we can't outrun them," she shouted. She pulled on the rope binding us together, and I was pulled by the wrists. Knowing I was not going to be able to talk Julie out of her idea, I tried to pull myself up onto the branch next to the one Julie was on.

"You hear that?" I asked during a pause in our climbing.

"Hear what? I hear nothing," Julie said, scanning the trees.

"Exactly—no gunshots," I confirmed. We sat, panting but relieved.

"So what now?" Julie asked. I knew I would have to wait before we climbed back down; my ankle was still aching slightly, but there was something else we could find out.

"Now we look at the map," I said. We made ourselves comfortable. We shifted so that I could move my hands enough to reach my bag. I pulled out the small mound of paper, and we rifled through it till we came across a small yellow envelope.

"This is it!" Julie said. "Now we can find out where the book is."

With shaking hands, I broke the seal and pulled out the paper inside. "It's a newspaper article!" I exclaimed. "I thought this was the map!"

Shoulders slumping, we decided to read the article anyway.

Talking Book: Myth or Reality!

Just when we thought the drama was over, not only have the rebels gained more followers, they have started their own myths!

"They are harping on about some talking book! They say it can grant wishes! It's ridiculous," one of the local residents says.

The myth is said by police to be the work of a Mrs. S., one of the rebels who will be evicted from the city this coming Friday. "All the evidence points to her. She is being forced to leave one of her sons in the city, and in the so-called myth, the book is said to have chosen to grant wishes after hearing a story about a mother losing her son. All the pieces fit."

The woman in question denies the claims that she made up the myth. She told the police that she has seen the book. She also said that the president of our city will never lay his pollution-ridden hands on it, as he does not possess enough brain cells to work out where it is. She finally added—before her arrest—that the book was hidden somewhere so obvious that no one would be able to use its last wish.

Police are looking into the mystery and are ready to confirm the fact that the story is just a myth. As of yet, there have been no sightings of the book, so the public can rest assured that it is not real.

(The picture to the left shows Mrs. S. at the Artefacts Museum in Blue Sea Bay.)

We sat in silence, both contemplating the news we had just read.

"It's not totally useless..." I said after a while. I knew I was trying to convince myself more than Julie. I had expected a map, and all I had gotten was a newspaper article.

"Well, if nothing else, we can keep it for the memories—you know, to show we found it," I dimly heard her say.

I looked closely at the picture. "Who is that woman?" I muttered to myself.

"Who, Mrs. S.?" Julie asked. "She's probably some old grandma or something." She stopped, her mouth dropping open in realisation. "Oh my, wow! She's one of our grandmas. Look! It says she was getting evicted!"

I looked at where she was pointing.

"Maybe..." she said slowly, "if we can find out whose grandma this is, we can find Mrs. S. and ask her where the book is!"

I thought about it. It sounded plausible but only just. "That's great," I said. "But there are loads of people with surnames that begin with S. It would take ages."

Julie pulled out her phone, opening up a blank page to type into. "Not necessarily," she said. "If we find out who has last names starting with S, we can deduce who she could be."

We were in no rush to go back down the tree. We didn't know if the man was still there, and it had started to rain. We had shelter under the leaves of our tree and were happy to stay there. Besides, we could look for Cleo and Terry easily from up there.

We decided to brainstorm ideas and came up with a list of twenty-two people whose last names began with S.

"Now we can knock people off our list," Julie said, going into full detective mode. I smiled and shook my head. She was about as logical in her plans as I was weird. (That means a lot.)

"You see, if Mrs. S. is a person's maternal grandma then we can knock that person off our list because that person would have inherited their name from their dad, not their mum," she reasoned. I nodded, impressed, and we began deducing.

Ten minutes later, we had a list of nine people.

"It's still a large number, but it's better," I said finally.

We saved the list and turned our concentration to the newspaper again.

"We should keep this," Julie announced, "just in case; it has proven useful." Nodding, I reached over to grab the paper, but the wind chose that moment to blow and carried the paper higher up the tree.

"Sugar Honey Iced Tea!" Julie exclaimed to herself. She climbed as high as she could but had to wait for me to hastily stuff my belongings into my bag because we were still tied together. Thankfully, my ankle had rested enough so we could chase our article in peace...and in rain.

Mud and leaves cascaded down on me from Julie's climb because she had to climb awkwardly (we were still tied together) and so shook the tree more. The wind started to pick up again, and we scrambled quicker, eager to get the paper before it was blown out of our reach.

"Almost got it!" Julie said as she stopped climbing.

She was balancing on her tiptoes on a branch, her hands stretched above her in an attempt to reach the paper. I dared not move, and so stayed ungracefully perched on a branch with my arms stuck up in front of me to allow Julie to carry on reaching for the paper. Looking down, I had to stifle a gasp; we were so high up!

The tops of other trees were dotted several metres below us, and the highest shrubs were quite a bit farther below that. I looked up once more. Julie was close. We would get it! Finally, her hand clasped around the bottom corner of the paper, but nature was against us at that moment.

The wind blew hard, and as her hand wrapped around the object, Julie's feet slipped, and she collapsed backwards, pulling me down with her.

"Ah!" The only sounds were our panicked yells as we desperately tried to latch onto anything that would stop our fall.

Leaves met me in the face; I fell almost in slow motion; the sun shone obliviously in the distance.

Branches.

I realised the rope between our wrists had caught onto a branch. I sighed in relief, thinking it would stop our fall. Instead, the rope snapped into two pieces, leaving me tangled in amongst leaves whilst Julie still plummeted towards the ground below.

"Grab onto something!" I shouted, managing to gain my bearings.

Arms flailing, she looked up at me desperately. It was as if I was watching her in slow motion. Her blond hair rose up and framed her terrified face.

All of a sudden, I heard a yell of "no!" and a blur ran through the trees, ploughing into Julie. Half catching, half running into her, the figure sent them both to the ground, but he broke her fall.

As the figure stood up, we both regarded him with a mixture of shock and joy.

1983

"Congratulations, it's a boy," the doctor said, handing her the baby. The woman, though exhausted, gladly took the baby and cradled him to her chest.

"He's so small," she murmured, looking up at her husband.

"Small but capable of a lot," he said, looking down at their son. The baby breathed contentedly as he slept.

"What's his name?" the nurse said, entering from behind the blue curtains.

The woman's husband smiled and replied, "Jack. His name is Jack."

Lily broke out of her reminiscence as a hurrying figure pushed past her to get to the door of the building to her right. Lily looked around, realising she had been standing still with a strange look on her face. She looked around.

"Come on! Hurry up, Jack!" she shouted to the small five-year-old that ran up to her.

"I'm running, Mummy. Wait!" the boy replied, a cheeky smile gracing his face.

Lily sighed. Whilst her husband, Tyler, insisted Jack was fast enough to become a champion runner when he was older, she still didn't think he was that fast. Of course, she didn't say anything; he was her son after all.

"Hurry up!" she said again, not daring to raise her voice too much. She spied the forest behind the prime minister's house, some way away.

Living undercover in the forest was not her first choice of lifestyle. She had always imagined living happily ever after in a little cottage with Tyler and Jack.

However, since the downfall of the Ecos, members had been found, one after the other, and exiled. In an attempt to escape, Lily had fled into the forest with Tyler, where they had lived for the last sixteen years.

She had tried to keep up regular correspondence with her parents. At first, they had been shocked to hear of her secrecy, but they had soon come to terms with the fact that she had done what she had done. They had had to get used to the fact that she now had to hide from the law. They did everything they could to keep her name off the map.

Perhaps the hardest part of the whole ordeal had been Jack. Whilst having a son was amazing, she could not afford to tell him the truth about herself. He was a five-year-old, and he could let something slip at any time. When he attended school, it was under Tyler's name. He was not registered anywhere under her name. But that wasn't the worst bit. The worst bit was making sure Jack fit in.

Since the arrest of the Ecos, Unistate had changed its name to Fun City. It was an attempt to mock Atro City, the city the Ecos had been exiled to. The whole Ecos business had made the residents of Fun City even surer that their polluting ways were right. If Jack went to school and disagreed with this belief, he would arouse suspicion. So to keep her family safe, Lily had to raise Jack as an Atro City hater and as a polluter, which she hated doing. She hoped that one day, she would be able to tell him the truth, but first, she had to make sure he was safe.

She shuddered, remembering the day of Trevor's trial. She hadn't been there, but she had seen the broadcast on TV. Everyone had seen it. It didn't matter that the family members may not have wanted their son's trial broadcast; they had housed the traitor, and that lost them their rights.

She had watched the trial in a daze. It was then that she had realised just how ruthless the people of Unistate (now Fun City) were. They had questioned Trevor again and again, regardless of his fear or tiredness. Lily's parents had also realised something that day. They had realised just how much danger their daughter was in.

Despite the events, the Ecos had still met up in their meet the next Sunday. They had been tense, as if waiting for disaster to strike. They were not wrong. No sooner had the last member entered the room than the door had been knocked open, and a man with a gun had entered. It had seemed that their secret was finally out for good.

Their first instinct had been to run. Not all being of athletic ability, some of the members had been caught. However, many had managed to escape. It was when she had returned home that Lily had really begun to see the impact of the Ecos.

Her parents had ushered her into the door quietly, looking outside in case anyone saw. They had given her a backpack, which they'd told her was stuffed with all she would need. Before she had the chance to question their actions, they had tearfully hugged her good-bye. She had hugged them and returned the sentiment, not entirely sure what was happening.

Then they had taken her into her back garden. Tyler had been waiting in one of her chairs, also with a backpack in his hands. It was him who had finally explained. Her parents had realised the danger she was in and had arranged for her to hide in a house in the forest until the events died down. Tyler and Lily had run out of her back garden and into the forest a few streets away. They had then travelled for days until they finally found their house. There, Tyler had told her about his parents and how they too knew of the events. Then Lily had settled into the house with him.

Then she waited for over sixteen years for the events to "blow over," as her dad had said.

A sudden gust of wind brought Lily out of her musings. She glanced around at the walking crowd of tourists, hoping she hadn't drawn any suspicion to herself as she stood silently. It wasn't very often that she ventured out of the forest. She usually left the venturing to her husband, who wasn't wanted by the police. When she did venture out, she tended to be very jumpy.

"Jack!" she called again. "Come on!" But when she glanced around, she couldn't see him.

"Jack?" she said, her heart thumping. She told herself not to panic. He's probably playing, she reminded herself. He was five after all. She checked her surroundings again, ducking her head against the strange looks people were giving her.

She glanced in the main reception area of the towering hotel to her right and peeked into the construction site on the left. Between the concrete blocks, mixing powder, and orange-clothed men, she made out no five-year-old boy.

She ventured down the street, not daring to run. She glanced in all the alleyways but saw no sign of him. At one point, she spied a group of children in an alleyway fighting with each other. As they neared the exit at the other end of the alley, people started to take notice. She rolled her eyes.

"Silly children, attracting attention to themselves," she muttered, taking another glance at them. However, at the second glance, she stopped dead. She knew that mop of blond hair only too well.

"Jack!" she half shouted, running down the alleyway. She couldn't believe he had gotten himself into a fight.

She neared the end of the alley and spied the road on the other side. Tall shops were cramped side by side, and narrow alleys, such as the one Lily ran through, divided them. Up ahead, past the main road, she saw golden sand stretching out beyond where she could see. It was littered with children playing and adults sunbathing. It was also littered with coast guards, who were starting to take a keen interest in the argument.

"Jack! Come on!" Lily said as she approached her son. She tugged on his arm, but he wouldn't budge.

"But Mummy!" the boy said, tears falling from his grey eyes. "He hurt me!"

Lily badly wanted to show the bully a lesson, but she couldn't risk being caught. She hated that her son would have to think she couldn't defend him.

"Jack," she said gently, bending down to whisper in his ear. "You know I can't."

The little boy sighed and wiped his tears. "Fine!" he said angrily. He pushed her away and stomped off down the alley. Lily straightened up to follow but found a figure in her way.

"Sorry!" the man exclaimed. "I'm just getting my son..." He trailed off as he pointed to none other than the boy Jack had been fighting.

"Yeah." Lily laughed nervously. "Minor scuffle." She had seen that man's dirty-blond hair before. The man bent down to pick up his son, and as he did so, his hair flopped messily over his face. As he rose with a strained look on his face, she recognised him. It was the man who had interrogated her!

"If you'll excuse me," she said, shuffling past him to where Jack stood sulkily at the end of the alley. She moved to the left to go around the man, then to the right, and then forwards. He too stepped right, then left, and then forwards, and they both ran into each other.

"Oops!" he laughed, bending down to retrieve the card that had fallen out of her purse. "Lily," he mused as he looked at the card whilst handing it back to her. "I met a girl called Lily once a…" He trailed off, looking closely at her. As dread settled in her stomach, his eyes widened.

"You!" he eventually said, jabbing a finger at her. His dark eyes hardened and shone with a ferocious new anger. He looked around himself quickly and then back at her.

"Eco! Eco! I've found an Eco!" he shouted at the top of his voice. Pushing past him, she ran down the alley, scooped Jack up into her arms, and carried on towards the woods.

1875

It was a bit of a blow to find out that Aunt Sareen didn't know where Lizzie's parents had moved to, but she could tell Lizzie and Charles where Lizzie used to live.

The two children left their belongings with Aunt Sareen, who Lizzie had told Charles she trusted. The two walked quickly down the street, keeping to the side of the street as they noted with dismay that Lizzie's picture was now printed in several newspapers. They tried to keep out of sight, and thankfully, years of avoiding people's sight and therefore their scorn seemed to have helped Lizzie stay out of sight, and Lizzie helped Charles keep out of the way.

Soon, they had made it to Lizzie's parents' house. Although he had never seen the place, Charles knew that this was it just by the way it looked. The walls were painted yellow, and he could see the faint outline of bananas around the corners of one of the windows. Although someone had tried to remove them, there were pink roses dotted along the yellow path that led to the door.

Maybe it was because there were lots of yellow things, or maybe it was the bananas, or maybe it was the pink roses, but this house screamed Lizzie's name. That was until they knocked. Then there was an actual scream of, "Thieves!"

Both Lizzie and Charles flinched.

"We are *not* thieves!" Lizzie said indignantly before the woman who had opened the door could shout again. "I used to live here, thank you very much."

This made the woman stop shouting, although now she was looking at the children in disgust.

"Oh, *you're* the child who was sent to the madhouse," the woman said disdainfully, trying to shut the door on them.

"Yes!" Lizzie said urgently, hearing the shouts of policemen from somewhere around the corner. For once, she was glad that everyone knew where Lizzie had been sent. "They sent me back; I got better, and I'm looking for my parents," she said quickly.

The woman looked down at them, and Charles could see that she didn't believe Lizzie but wanted to get rid of her.

"So they left without you," she said. "That's not surprising, considering where their daughter *went*. They're gone now, to Unistate."

The shouts of the policemen had gotten closer, but Lizzie and Charles had all the information they needed.

Ignoring the woman and her disdain, the two children once again ran.

They shot past the left street and skidded around the corner by the bakery. Lizzie ran into the bakery, went straight up the stairs, grabbed the bread and water—forgetting the one pound—and sailed through the window, which Charles had run under whilst Lizzie was inside. He caught her, and the two set off over the fence.

Curving around the bushes at the back of the fence, the two children took the first alley they saw and ran as far away from the buildings as possible. They came to another fence, some bushes, and a rather pink dog. However, they neared the last fence, which told them that they were leaving the town, and vaulted over it.

It turned out the town was at the top of a very large hill. Charles managed to catch his footing thanks to a helping hand from Lizzie. However, her momentum was too great and pulling Charles back hadn't helped it. Lizzie's foot slid forwards, and she went tumbling down the hillside.

Charles ran after her, jumping over the fallen trees and the awkward ridges. He heard the police behind him and a plane above him, and he saw another bomb in front of him. He rushed faster. He had to get to her before the bomb did.

Then hands grabbed him from behind as the policemen caught up.

"It's OK," the man who had him said stiffly. "You don't need to play hero anymore."

Charles struggled in his arms, wanting nothing more than to save Lizzie, but he couldn't. He knew that, and he also knew that if he tried and survived, then he would be arrested too. If he stayed, he wouldn't be arrested because people would think that Lizzie had just forced Charles to go with her. Either way, Lizzie was gone.

So he stilled. He let the officer set him down and let him think he had been running to catch Lizzie, not help her. The man told him to turn around, that the bomb explosion was going to be bright, but he couldn't. He watched in a sort of transfixed horror as the bomb got lower and lower towards the bottom of the hill.

And then there was a bang, and a surge of dust rippled out in all directions. Heat blasted him in the face, and the dust got into his eyes. Trees shook all around him, and nearer the bottom of the hill, they fell, shaking the desolate ground. But Charles didn't hear any of it. Charles didn't see any of it. Lizzie was down there. That was all he knew.

It seemed wrong that the dust could just settle, that petrified silence and shocked stillness was all that remained afterwards. Charles couldn't believe Lizzie was gone; he wouldn't believe it.

Suddenly, he was on his feet. He was running down the hill, towards the damage, towards Lizzie.

He was at the bottom of the hill pulling at tree trunks by the time anyone caught up with him. He hadn't realised he had tears falling down his cheeks; he hadn't realised that he had been calling her name till a hand clamped over his, and he was pulled through a gap between two trunks, leaving a burnt shoe behind.

2029

Terry sat still, wincing as I treated the cut on his ankle. He and Julie had been involved in a long conversation since we had realised he had been her saviour. Although I had been chosen to find the book, they both knew more than I did, and so I left the planning to them.

"North would be the best way to go," Terry started. "No...south—" I wrapped his leg with my bandage.

"We should really find the rest of the map first," I cut in, calling it a *map* even though it was a newspaper article. It was easier to refer to it that way.

When Julie had fallen from the tree, she had kept a firm grasp on the map, but she said the map had been tightly coiled around a branch and so had ripped in half and flown away.

"What chance is there of finding it though?" Julie countered, supporting Terry as he tried a few steps.

"Well, we don't know where we are, so we may as well just explore for now and hope for the best," I finished for them.

Terry had eaten the last of my sandwiches, meaning we would have to rely on berries and water for now. We still hadn't found Cleo, and I was getting worried.

"So what if police men arrested Cleo?" Terry scoffed. "He was probably getting us arrested any way; we just got *him* arrested first."

Julie and I looked at each other. We hadn't let ourselves consider the possibility that he had been arrested, but now the idea seemed plausible. I remembered what the guards had said: "We get the post—the right to condemn him!"

"But they couldn't have been talking about Cleo, right?" I said apprehensively. "They couldn't have found him; he disappeared right after the explosion."

There was silence for a few minutes as we trudged through the forest. The mud squelched under our feet, and my socks began to get wet.

"It *could* be a trap…" Julie ventured. "The police men might have been lying about getting to condemn Cleo. The mayor could have planned it. The mayor would do something like that. He hates Atro City, and he would do anything to get back at us, especially if we have the book."

I thought to myself and then said, "I see no real reason to go back. If we stay out of sight, it would lead the police to think we don't care about Cleo, and therefore, he can't have helped us that much. If we go save him, it will prove he helped us, and we will effectively be putting him in prison."

Terry and Julie nodded.

"That does seem plausi—" Terry stopped. In front of us, casually placed deep in the forest, was a cottage. It looked like one of those cottages you expect to see on a Christmas card, only several thousand years older and way more worn down.

The windows were fogged up with age, but a warm yellow glow emerged from within. We stood frozen, not sure whether we should continue forwards or go around. Then a man stepped out of the door. He had a kind smile but hard eyes, and he pushed us into his house kindly before we had the chance to run.

☩

"So you are the ones who convinced my son to go rogue," the man said as he offered us each a cup of tea.

He wore a smart grey suit, like the ones my dad wore to special events. He had short spiky hair and cold black eyes.

"Do you mean Cleo?" I asked, taking the cup but with no intention of drinking from it.

The man smiled warmly, which made him look like Cleo for a moment. I almost found it hard to be suspicious of him. He handed us each some biscuits, and I ventured a bite.

Although this man was a relative of Cleo's, I found it hard to warm to him. Cleo may have been nice to us, but could I vouch for his relatives?

"Mmm. These are really good!" Terry said, echoing the thoughts of Julie and I. The man handed him two more biscuits.

"I thank you for what you did," the man finally said. We assumed he was talking about getting Cleo to help. "I have been treated as an outcast for years; now maybe the truth will be uncovered," he continued, and Julie nodded in agreement.

"Now, if we succeed, we can teach Fun City a good lesson!" she added, referring to her anger at Fun City for all they had done. The man smiled in agreement.

"Yes…" he said. "There *will* be lessons for people." I didn't like the way he said that. For a second, his eyes had looked mean. I held back a shiver. The way he said *lessons* implied a crueller meaning.

"Come," he said to Terry, seeing he had finished his biscuits. "I will get you some more." Without thinking, Terry got up to go. I watched him with a bad feeling settling in my stomach.

"Something isn't right," Julie said, the minute the man was out of earshot. I nodded.

"I know; why would he be glad we got his nephew arrested?"

Julie's brows furrowed. "It's not just that," she said, pulling something from her pocket. "Look what I found in the hallway." She showed me the object in her hand. It was the newspaper we thought we had lost forever. Somehow, the man had gotten possession of it.

Julie hastily stuffed the paper into her pocket as we heard footsteps. The man came back into the room, smiling. His smile was devoid of any warmth.

"Where's Terry?" I asked. The man smiled once more.

"He's being taken care of."

Julie and I looked at each other.

The man said, "Why don't you come with me, Kayla?" I got up, not wanting to refuse and put him on guard. As I followed him out the room, I mouthed to Julie, "Find Terry." She nodded, and I walked up the stairs.

He led me into the far room. It was small, only a boxroom without windows. Having no choice, I walked in, mentally sighing when he stood in front of the door and sealed my only exit. The doorway was filled with newspapers. Old and new ones stood stacked in piles on the tables and the cabinets and the floor, leaving just enough room to walk.

"Thought these might help," the man said, but I had an inkling he was just trying to separate the three of us.

"Why?" I asked anyway. I might as well gather as much information as I could.

"Because these contain all the news," he replied, "for the last ten years. You may find some clues."

Looking at him hesitantly, I picked up the top newspaper on the nearest pile. He smiled smugly as I did so, as if he had wanted me to pick it up. The paper had today's date on it and the words *copy one*. Internally, I wondered how he could have gone to the Fun City shops, bought the *first* newspaper, and come back, because it was still somewhat early in the morning. I read it anyway.

Traitor Boy Arrested

This morning at nine o'clock, Cleo Stevenson was arrested and charged with being a traitor to Fun City. After he pled not guilty, a case was set up to investigate the matter.

"He is most definitely guilty," a police officer revealed. "It adds up. Years ago, he lost an uncle to the rebellion by the people of Atro City. It makes sense that he should feel resentful and help his uncle's people years later to get back at us."

Police found Cleo in the forests by the prime minister's mansion shortly after the fuel tank exploded inside said building. Police suspect he was going to find his grandfather, who is said to live in a small cottage there.

We are unsure as of yet what the punishment will be, but rest assured, it will be harsh. The traitor will not be allowed in Fun City again.

The mayor of Fun City sent a message to the so-called outsmarter girl:

"Come, and rescue your boy, who deserves to be exiled with your scum rather than stay with us. If you do not, we will leave him to starve. Bring us back the book. Only then will we let him go. It will be a trade—the book for the boy. His life is in your hands. You have forty-eight hours."

More news on the case can be seen on Channel B.

I stared at the paper in shock. Cleo had been arrested, or at least that is what the paper had said. I tried to stand by my earlier thoughts of leaving him be, but my heart said otherwise. If he is Cleo Stevenson...can you leave him? I asked myself. The answer was no. If he was who this paper said he was, I would be just as bad as the Fun City people if I left him behind.

Looking at the man briefly, I saw he wore a sinister, smug smile. Again, my brain told me this was a trick. The newspaper was fake. How else could he have gotten the very first copy?

I looked at the picture by the newspaper article. It showed the forest by the prime minister's mansion and Cleo being cuffed by policemen. But in the background, there was something I recognised.

It was a cottage. The same one I was in now. And if I squinted, I could see a second one, some way behind the first. That was where Grandpa Stevenson lived. Grandpa Stevenson—I would have to rescue him too.

Behind me, the man looked at me knowingly, as if he revelled in the chaos the paper had created in my mind, as if he understood the truth this article had just unearthed.

I would like to say I felt like every other hero in the books—that my troubled life finally made sense—but I didn't. My life hadn't been troubled. I had both parents and even my grammie. I had never been told stories as a child about my heroic ancestors that inspired me to take on the lifelong path of a hero. I had never fallen prey to any weird looks or strange gut feelings that were clues to my past.

I was normal. I had grown up happy and oblivious to the secrets that had been hiding in my family for decades.

"You will save him…won't you?" the man asked, almost telling me rather than asking. I nodded, not trusting myself to talk. "The thing is," he continued, "I don't believe you." He pulled a small knife out of his pocket. "So I'm sure you can forgive me for this."

I ducked just in time as he swung and knocked a pile of newspapers over.

"Julie! Terry! Run!" I shouted, hoping they would have the sense to just leave. I stepped back and fell over a pile of newspapers. Picking up as many as possible, I hurled them at his face. He brought his hands up. I scrambled for the newspaper with today's date and ran out the room, pushing him farther in and closing the door for good measure.

"Julie, where are you?" I asked as I reached the bottom of the stairs. She came running out of the first door and motioned for me to follow her.

The room we ran into was nothing like the living room. It was dark and grey. Two chairs sat in the centre, and Terry was tied to one of them, with industrial-strength tape over his mouth.

"Quick," I said, pulling out the knife. "I don't think he'll be gone for long."

With shaking hands, I tried to cut the rope, and together, Julie and I ripped the tape off his face.

"Mmm…mmm…mmm. Aaaaahhhhhhhh!" Terry yelled as his mouth was freed.

"Stay still," I chided as I tried to get the knife through the ropes. I cut faster as I heard footsteps from the stairs. One hand free, and one to go. "Almost there…" I said as I started on his last hand. The door opened with a bang.

"You're not going anywhere." The man was back.

Julie nodded to us, letting us know she would buy us some time. "You don't want to kill us," she said bravely.

"And why is that?" he asked smugly. "Because my son will die? I couldn't care less! He's always been a green boy. Gets it from his grandma, I expect. He was stupid to think he could help."

The knife cut through the last rope, and I stood up, leaving the knife behind the chair so the man didn't see it and just attack. Terry acted as if he was still in his ropes.

"But what if we run?" I asked.

He smirked once more. "Then you leave your friend tied up."

"No, they won't," Terry said angrily, shooting out of the chair and tackling the man, taking him by surprise.

Terry, Julie, and I ran from the building and leaned against the door to stop the man from emerging.

"This won't hold forever," I said.

"Are we going to leave the city?" Julie returned. I nodded.

"Then...we know where the walls are," Terry finished, and planning as one, we ran.

The chase was three to one, so it should have been easy, but we refused to lose sight of each other and ran half our normal speed in order to do so. Every so often, one of us would have to stop and fend off the madman, but we kept on running.

Some way through running, I felt as if I were on autopilot. My head was running through the same instructions—run, check, fight, run. And for what seemed like a large portion of the day, that was what we did.

As time went on, I was sure we were only doing a fast walk. Our enemy was still on our heels, like a rabid dog, coming in for the bite. Up ahead, we saw the towering bronze walls. Faded and rusty, they weren't nearly as majestic a sight as those at the front. We had reached the border, but now we were trapped.

"Quick! Look for a door!" Terry yelled. We parted, scanning left and right for an escape. Somehow, we all knew there was no door.

Finally, the man caught up with us. Weary from running, I made a mistake and allowed him to kick the knife out of my hand, and he made the first strike. I ducked just in time, recognising his attack-heavy fighting style. I didn't want to fight him. I knew I would be back in these forests, and I didn't want an enemy to meet me when I returned.

I turned and ran, leading him on a wild Kayla chase. I was tired from running and hoped he would soon tire and falter. Suddenly, I turned and punched him. I caught him squarely in the stomach. He doubled over, and I made my way back to the wall.

"Guys...guys?" I called. They were nowhere to be seen, and the madman would be back soon.

A hand dropped in front of me from the tree.

"Hurry, and get up!" Julie called. I took her hand, and she pulled me up.

Running away was slower, but we navigated from atop the trees to get back to the wall. From below, I could hear the steps of the man; he wanted to turn us in.

"We're at the wall; climb over," Terry whispered. Our chaser was directly below us, and we had to make a move.

Carefully, Julie made the transition. She made it onto the top of the wall, but the branch on the other side bent worryingly as she went over to the other side.

I was next. Following the same movements Julie had made, I stood on the wall. Grabbing hold of the branch, I slid over.

The branch bent. I slid quicker.

The branch creaked. I stopped.

The branch broke.

I went tumbling to the ground and would have probably broken a few hundred bones had it not been for Julie and her quick thinking to plough into me the same way Terry had her.

"Kayla! Are you OK?" I heard from the other side of the fence.

"I'm fine," I called back, but Terry wasn't.

"Finally caught ya!" a second voice called. I heard the sounds of a scuffle. It seemed the man had found us out.

Feeling helpless, we waited to see the outcome of the scuffle. A few minutes later, a figure jumped down off the wall and greeted us with a smug smirk.

1875

"Get off. Get off!" Charles screamed, kicking at the person holding him. He felt a hand try to cover his mouth, so he kicked harder.

"Ow!" He heard the girl cry as his kick hit her. He smiled triumphantly, then stopped.

He knew that voice.

"Lizzie!" he hissed, looking back towards the hand. He almost cried at the sight. Her arms were burnt slightly, and soot covered her face, apart from two hand-shaped clear patches over her eyes.

Her eyes were watering, probably because of the heat that just washed over her from the bomb. The bomb. The one that should have killed her. Suddenly, he felt his legs give way, and she helped him to the ground. She dragged him away from the gap in the trunks he had been pulled through, and he realised that they were resting on a ridge sticking out the steep hill, a similar ridge to the one they had hidden under to escape a bomb only that morning.

"You're alive!" he managed. He laughed and hugged her, not caring about the fact that he had cut his ankle falling between the branches. "How are you alive?" he finally asked.

"I hit a tree and stumbled back under the little ridge," she said, croaking from the soot. Charles realised that this little ridge she was under was more like a cave.

"I remembered, Charles," Lizzie whispered. "I remembered how I got to Victon."

And sitting hidden from the police under two tree trunks and a hill, she whispered her story.

2029

"No!" Julie gasped as she took in the sight of Cleo's dad.

"Where's Terry?" I demanded. I couldn't hear anything beyond the walls.

The man smirked. "Your friend is no man for up-close fighting. It was easy to take him down."

My heart sank into my stomach as I exchanged glances with Julie. The man could very well be right; up-close fighting was not Terry's thing.

"Uh, Kayla," Julie murmured. "One of your weird plans would be good right now."

I searched my mind for anything that I could use. Quickly, I formed a half-baked plan. "You won't do anything to us!" I said loudly. I put a hand in my bag as if to pull out a knife. The man replied by fisting his hands in front of him. "Are you sure you wish to do this?" I asked, bluffing.

With the hand in my bag, I fiddled with the rope. Cleo's father punched. Hoping I knew how to make a lasso out of rope well enough, I pulled the rope out of the bag.

I met his punch as it came, putting the loop of the rope around his wrist. He kicked, ignoring the rope as a small hindrance. I jumped the kick and threw the rope over the wall. The man brought his hand forwards to punch, but he never got far enough. From the other side of the wall, someone pulled the rope taut. The rope pulled the man up by his arm as a person climbed up the other side. Eventually, Cleo's father was pulled up and over the other side of the wall. Terry, having climbed the other side, dropped the rope on the other side of the wall as Cleo's father ran away with it.

"Terry!" Julie said happily. She had been somewhat confused by my actions. The three of us shared smug grins and turned together to look beyond the walls.

Not far off, we could see our home. The trees rose high and mighty, giving the barest glimpses of houses. The train tracks ran far around the trees and on towards Blue Sea Bay. The sight of our neighbouring bay stirred my memory, as if the place was important, but I couldn't remember why.

I thought of my parents and what they would be doing at this time. Dad would be at home with Grammie, having his daily cup of tea. Mum would most likely be out, maybe at the little bakery on Elm's Olden. In some way, I was tempted to forget the book and run home. But then I realised that as tempting as that sounded, I couldn't return home and let the people who had trusted me suffer for the sins of Fun City.

"We can't stay here for long," Julie said, realising that we were feeling the urge to walk right home, as she was. Tearing our eyes from the scene, we walked alongside the walls for a mile or two, just in case our chaser should come over and try to find us.

"So what now?" Julie asked as we flopped onto the grass.

"I guess we get the book and go home once and for all." Terry sighed.

I felt anxious; I knew I should tell them what I had planned.

"Guys, I think we should go back for Cleo—" I started, but I didn't get very far.

"No!"

"Why should we?"

"What do you mean go back!"

My heart began to sink. If this was their attitude now, what would they say when they found out my plan for Cleo's grandpa?

"I think it would be good. I mean, sure, Cleo chose to help us, and we didn't force him to, but whatever he chose, we benefited from it. So isn't it a bit mean to leave him behind?" I tried, hoping they would agree. I didn't think I would know what to do if they disagreed with me. But one thing was for sure, I was going to get Cleo, and Mr. Stevenson as well.

Julie and Terry looked at each other. I could tell my demand confused them, and I hated keeping secrets from them, but this was something I had to do, even if they couldn't know why.

"Fine." Terry eventually consented, studying me with creased eyebrows. I couldn't quite meet his eyes. "We will go back for Cleo. But what if it is a trick?"

"We go back anyway," I said, marvelling at the certainness in my voice. In truth, I had no idea whether the paper was a trick, and it almost terrified me to think about what would happen to my friends if it turned out to be fake.

"What about the deal? Do we actually give the prime minister the book in return for Cleo?" Julie asked, her voice turning hateful upon saying the boy's name.

"We'll think about that when the time comes," I returned. So far, I had them convinced.

"Ugh! I just want to get this thing over and done with!" Terry sighed. Unlike most of the boys I knew, he valued fighting from a distance, and so this up-close searching was not his forte. However, he had a knack for geography and was a valuable asset. Of course, I couldn't think of my friends only as tools. We had been training together since we were mere three-year-olds, and so we felt as if we knew everything about each other. In fact, as I watched Terry lean against the walls of Fun City, I could almost guess the turmoil going through his head. He had a little sister at home and a rugby club. It was somewhat obvious that he missed them both.

Julie on the other hand, hated rugby, which pained our gym teacher to no end, as she was utterly convinced Julie could be a star player if she so pleased.

Whilst this may seem typical of a teenage girl, Julie loved the outdoors and grew up with three brothers. She could scale a tree in under a minute if she wanted to, which of course aggravated our gym teacher because Julie won't join the climbing club either.

"So where is this book?" Terry eventually asked, breaking the weary silence that had hung between us.

I sighed and explained our theory that Mrs. S. from the newspaper would know.

"But we didn't find out who Mrs. S. is," Julie finished. I didn't want to say that I knew who Mrs. S. was.

"Can I see the paper?" Terry requested. Slowly, I took it out of my bag and handed it to him.

For a few minutes, we sat in silence, watching as Terry read the paper and examined every sentence for any clue. "Mrs. S.," he muttered. "She would help us." He sighed. "But we don't know who she is."

Eventually, he finished the article and looked at the bottom. His eyes slowly widened. "Guys, we've got a lead," he said. We jumped up, looking at each other in disbelief. How had we missed something?

He pointed to the picture in the corner. "Look at the caption," he instructed. I looked down and knew where we had to go. It read, "Mrs. S. at Blue Sea Bay."

1983

Lily couldn't believe she had gotten caught by the police. As she sat in her cell, her mind reprimanded her again and again as she considered her own stupidity. Her only success at the moment was that she had managed to get Jack out of the way before she had been caught. Not that it had been hard. He had been angry with her for not fighting for him and so had been happy to run away from her.

Lily glanced around her room. A small bed graced one corner and a table, the other. The wall between them housed a single window, adorned with bars and restrained by curtains. The last wall contained bars running from left to right. Cold and silver, they made the space glow as the moon shone on them. Beyond the bars, the room faded into inky blackness. Lily shivered. Although she didn't expect to be here long, she didn't like it. She didn't like the fact that there was no glass in the window, she didn't like that she had had to hide for sixteen years, she didn't like the camera in the corner of the room, and she most certainly didn't like the fact that there was a person watching her at the other end.

She sighed. Whether she liked it or not, she would have to stay for a few days until the police gave her a trial. *If* they gave her a trial. Knowing them, she wouldn't be surprised if they exiled her without any formality. With that happy thought, she lay down in the small bed and got ready to sleep.

⅄

"ID one four seven nine five. You have post!"

It took Lily a few seconds to realise that the ID being called out was hers. She hurriedly stood up and reached her hand out of her bars. The letter slipped into her hand, and she pulled it back in again.

Now that it was daytime, she could see more of where she was. Six more cells exactly like Lily's ran along the wall next to hers. Desks lined the opposite wall, piled with papers.

Lily hadn't as of yet met the criminals in the adjoining cells, but she had heard their moaning and complaints for the past three days. Saying they were grating on her nerves would be the biggest understatement since Josh called himself tall.

Her smile faded; she missed her old friends. But she would meet them soon.

What the police didn't know was that Lily was *still* an Eco member. Just because they were exiled didn't mean the Ecos had given up. They had kept in close correspondence with those still in Fun City and had wreaked all sorts of havoc.

Lily was one of the people who had been feeding information from inside Fun City. She was one of three Ecos still left the in Fun City area. Now that she had been caught, she had been told by the Ecos in Atro City to make as much trouble as possible for Fun City. She needed to cause a disturbance so the remaining two Ecos could restore their covers and have less chance of getting caught.

Rolling her eyes as she heard her neighbour complain that she never got letters, Lily sat on her bed. Turning the letter over, she froze.

> To L. L., ID 14795
> Fun City Prison Centre for Dangerous Criminals
> 123 Dolobab Road
> HG-6K-O8

It said *L. L.* She knew what that meant. This letter was from the Ecos. Glancing at the camera in the corner, Lily discretely turned herself so the letter would be out of view, and then she opened it. She was presented with a normal letter that looked as if it was from her mother, but was not fooled. Lily knew that the Ecos would hide their message for fear of the government reading her letters. She didn't bother reading the letter, but went straight to the postcard attached. It was a normal laminated postcard.

Too normal.

Pretending to wash her hands in the basin provided at the corner of the room, Lily wet her hands with hot water and held the postcard. The laminate began to fall off as the glue was wet. The picture from the postcard, which was only held in place by the laminate, fell off, revealing a message written in tiny handwriting underneath.

To L. Lily,

It has been quite a few months since we have needed to ask for your expertise in causing trouble. However, our plans are in danger of being discovered, and so we must act fast.

A few months ago, a runaway from another country showed up at the borders of our city. He claimed to have a book that can grant wishes. He told us that he had heard of Atro City and how we accepted other exiles to live with us. He mentioned that he had run away because the people in his previous home had all thought him mad for believing in a magic book.

Obviously, being outcasts ourselves, we sympathised and accepted him, but we were wary of his book. Recognising this, he offered us proof and showed us how the book works.

After having grasped the immense power of the book, we sought to protect it. However, the prime minister of Fun City had somehow come to know what we possessed. Luckily, we managed to hide the book from him, but we are unsure how long our success will last.

This is where you come in, L. L. Here in Atro City, we accept new ideas and value them. However, in Fun City, ideas such as being eco-friendly and having magic books are ridiculed. We know that if the prime minister's search became public, the book would be ridiculed, and he would be forced to stop, or at least slow down, his search. We

would like you, as our chief mischief weaver, to make sure the whole
city finds out about a magic book that grants wishes.

Best of luck.
The Ecos

Lily sat back and took a deep breath. So much had been going on in Atro
City! She reread the letter to be sure of what had happened. They had found
a book, and it was her job to make sure everyone knew about it so the prime
minister couldn't look for it and it would stay hidden.

She smiled. It was obvious that either Josh or Willow had come up with
the plan. It was equally as confusing as it was brilliant, so it was sure to
work! She could see how it would work. If the public knew about the book,
the prime minister would have to forfeit his search to keep his reputation.
Vaguely, Lily wondered where the book was hidden.

Shrugging, she folded the letter up; she didn't need to know. She only
needed to do her work.

⚓

Lily pushed her hair out of her face and sighed. There was a shuffling from
behind her, and she turned to look behind herself at the other criminals that
had been brought into the room. Although they had all been deemed the
most obedient and least dangerous, they all looked pretty scary to Lily.

There was Sam, a woman with self-cut black hair and eyebrow piercings.
There was Loaf, a big man who was probably square enough to pass for a loaf
of bread. There were also Jim, Toby, and Catlo, three brothers who were each
scarier than the next. Then there was Lily. She was quite possibly the smallest
and the most human looking of the group. And today, she had the pleasure of
going on a prison trip with the five other criminals.

At first, Lily hadn't understood why prison members would be allowed
on educational trips. Then, after having overheard a conversation between
two policemen, she had realised that like all things, it was for Fun City's ben-
efit and not the criminals'. It just so happened that Fun City's reputation had
gone down dramatically in the time since Lily had gotten arrested. Fun City

would allow some criminals to go on these educational trips to prove that it had been on top of criminal activity and could control the criminals.

That was why Lily planned to use this opportunity to embarrass Fun City as much as possible.

Lily smiled as she watched the clouds above her. She planned to make plenty of trouble.

⚔

Tcc! The buttons of Lily's overall clipped together with a snap. She sighed as she looked at her reflection in the mirror of the prison's changing room. Her red overall overpowered her form, making her look sickly and pale. She turned; it didn't matter how she looked because they would exile her anyway.

She had known that she would be exiled, but she hadn't really processed that fact. Inside, she had been hoping there was a way she could stay, not that she knew why. In Fun City, she was an outcast; at least in Atro City, she wouldn't have to hide. But Fun City was the only home she had known; how could she leave that?

A uniformed man broke into her thoughts. He had dark skin and brandished his weapon proudly.

"They will see you now," he said. Lily took a deep breath; this was it—her trial.

⚔

This was it. Lily looked at the sprawling city that stretched out behind her. The white-marble temples contrasted with the rusted bricks of the houses. The windowed buildings reflected the sun's late glow.

By the silver gates of the city, a huge concrete space spanned out in a grey aisle from the gates. This area was used by special figures entering and exiting the city. On that day, it was crowded with people as they stepped up to see the traitor exiled.

"Ladies and gentlemen!" The prime minister's voice rang throughout the space. The wind carried it right across to those perching on roofs some roads away. "Today, you will witness a cleansing." He turned to Lily. "People like this dirty our city with their green ways. We don't want to be green!" He gestured up at the white fog, as if it were a good thing. "We don't want to be a horrible green colour…we want to stay pearly white!"

Cheers arose from the crowd. They were so oblivious to the danger of their ways.

"By ridding our sweet city of these dirty people," the prime minister continued, "we shall be assuring our lives!" More cheers arose, and Lily rolled her eyes. What silly people they were.

Lily scanned the crowd, bored of listening to the speech. The prime minister could lie as much as he wanted, but she wouldn't listen. Glancing around, she scanned the faces of those watching.

She saw her old neighbour Neville, Margret, the shop lady, Bill Tompson, and Tyler.

Tyler!

She looked over once more to see Tyler sitting innocently atop a tree branch, holding a sleeping figure in his right arm. He looked straight at her, smiling as she noticed him.

"What are you doing!" she mouthed to him, making sure everyone else was preoccupied with the prime minister's speech. In response, he merely grinned. He waved a finger, signalling her to wait. Then he proceeded to fiddle with something inside his pocket. Looking around to make sure no one was looking, he flicked it out of his palm.

Gusts of wind carried it up and over in loop-the-loops, and finally, it landed on the ground right in front of her feet. Checking to make sure no one was paying any attention to her, she bent down, pretending to tie her shoes, and picked up the object. Looking at it, she recognised it as a bookmark. Written on the front were the words "We shall see each other again, if not through our eyes, then through our future."

She looked up at him questioningly, but he only smiled, as if saddened by what he saw. "Good-bye," he mouthed, and then she was herded away by policemen into a car and taken away from all she had ever known.

2029

The train that ran around Terry's, Julie's, and my home city could make it from one border to another in three hours. Which was good, seeing as we had barely forty-eight hours left to find this book, go back to Fun City, get Cleo, and manage to keep the book, and for me to get Grandpa Stevenson.

The conductor let us on the train without any problems. We told him we needed to board the train because we needed to go to Blue Sea Bay to find the book, and he told us to hop on for free. It was good seeing as we had no money anyway.

We sat in silence, watching the trees pass us by. It felt good to see the lush green of our home again. Through the leaves, we occasionally saw children playing or a lone house. However, the three hours seemed to go too quickly.

Finally, the train ground to a stop, and we left our home for the second time.

"Bye, thank you, Mr. Haily," we chorused. He waved to us from the conductor's seat.

"Bye...and...oh! Kayla, you dropped something!" he said as the train took off again. I looked down at ground. It was the bookmark. I didn't see the point of keeping it, but my grammie had insisted it was important, so I slipped it into my dagger's sheath on my arm.

"So we are at Blue Sea Bay," Julie said. "What now?"

Shrugging, I crossed the border. "We explore, I guess."

I had only been to Blue Sea Bay once on a trip to the museum, but I'm pretty sure it wasn't this crowded. If I had remembered that it was, I would have brought a big sharp stick to jab all the people who, for some reason, seemed to think I was someone they could walk through. It was as if I had a KICK ME sign on my back in neon colours that the whole world could see.

We walked along a road in Blue Sea Bay and about after twenty minutes of navigating our way across the road, we finally got to the opposite side of the street, where we had a much-deserved sit down outside one of the cafés.

"I guess exploring won't be the best option." I was forced to admit defeat as we put our bags on the table.

"If it's all the same to you, I'd rather not be trampled on by crowds of people," Terry agreed.

Julie sighed next to me. "So what do we do then?" she asked. We looked around at what we could see. Over the crowds of people, we saw skyscrapers in the distance. Parallel to the beach and opposite where we were sitting, cafés and small shops lined the road, hoping to attract the attention of the busy people.

However, it was the building I could see behind the row of shops that caught my eye. It was possibly the biggest museum I had seen; its tall red bricks rose high, closing into a dome at the top so it looked as if it were reflecting the sun. Two thin towers of rock rose on either side, both inscribed with symbols and pictures. Although it was behind a row of shops, I could still see the tops of the entrance doors, which rose halfway up the structure and were carved out of dark wood.

"Guys—" I started to say.

"Oh look!" Terry interrupted, smirking at me. "I know that look. It's weird-plan time."

Punching him playfully on the shoulder, I laughed as he fell sideways off the chair. Glaring at me, he got up.

"What's that called?" I asked, pointing to the museum. I knew it from somewhere.

"Oh that," Julie said, ready at once with her geographical knowledge. "It's the Artefacts Museum. Apparently, it is one of the best in the country. It has statues, fossils, clothes, and—"

"Books?" I interrupted.

Julie looked at me. "Yeah…books." She and Terry looked at each other.

"Surely you don't think it's in there?" Terry said dubiously, but the pieces had already started clicking in my head.

"Look," I said excitedly, pulling out the paper we had taken from Fun City. "Mrs. S. says that the paper was hidden in an obvious place—"

"And where is more obvious than a museum?" Julie finished, though she didn't sound completely convinced. "That's all good, Kayla, but why this museum? There could be loads of museums in Blue Sea Bay that—"

"Kayla's right," Terry interrupted suddenly.

"She is?" Julie exclaimed.

"I am?" I asked. I hadn't expected them to agree so easily, especially not Terry, who liked to know what he was walking into.

"You are," Terry assured me. He pointed to the picture next to the news article. "Look at the picture," he instructed.

With our brows furrowed, we studied the picture, and slow smiles came to our faces.

"Picture taken at the Artefacts Museum," I read aloud slowly. I looked up. "This is brilliant! Now we know where to look."

Julie started to smile as well, but Terry shook his head. "No." He sighed. "Look behind Mrs. S." Looking towards where his finger was pointing, we squinted and made out the shape of a book.

"Do you really think that's the book?" Julie asked suspiciously. "It seems too easy."

"It is the one," I said. I couldn't tell them how I knew, because they would never believe me. However, I knew who Mrs. S. was, and if I knew anything about her, it's that she would have purposely been interviewed in front of the book, not only to serve as a clue for its seekers but also to make silent fools out of those in Fun City who couldn't find it.

We decided against buying tickets and then hiding in the museum until after it was closed. First of all, we didn't know the museum well enough to hide in it, and secondly, we had no money. That left us with one option: we would sneak in.

We scouted the streets around the museum, finding out anything we could about the museum and, more importantly, about how it was laid out.

The streets were bigger than we thought. They were wide enough for three lanes, and it was a mission in itself not to get buried in the crowd. Several times, we had to drag Julie away from various shops selling sports clothes, and once, we even had to drag Terry away from an all-you-can-eat buffet that was giving away free samples. Though, between you and me, I may have taken a sample or two.

Finally, the sky became a mixture of blues, and the museum closed. Signalling to each other to be quiet, we made our way to the main doors. Right when we were just about to test the lock, the doors opened with a bang.

Jumping back in shock, I pulled Terry with me behind the closest tower. Julie was not so lucky, and the school-trip pupils who exited looked at her in confusion.

"Come, dear," a woman—the teacher—said to her, mistaking her for a student. "Come on with us then." And Julie had no choice but to follow. Terry and I looked at each other in horror but had no time to go back. We had to go in before the doors closed and locked us out.

The entrance hall was just as glorious as the front of the museum. Our footsteps echoed dangerously loudly as we made our way to the centre. Rounded corridors made their ways out from a wide, round room like tunnels, and glass boxes on stands held glimpses of what lay within them.

A dark-red light shone up from lights in the floor, making the room look as if blood lined the tall ceiling.

"Come on; this way," Terry said, walking towards the tunnel on the right. We hadn't been able to see more than a few feet inside it before, and we walked in awe.

I used to think the library was big, but this corridor lined with dusty novels and sacred tomes was much larger. There was an opus or two and even a kind of rock engraved with Egyptian hieroglyphs. Soon, the corridor opened up into a large round room, much like the entrance hall. We looked at each other and stepped in.

The perimeter was lined with glass boxes, which each encased one rarity after another.

Using our torch and the newspaper, as we had planned, we managed to work out where Mrs. S. must have been standing in the picture and, therefore, where the book was. We crouched down, looking in the glass case at the book that lay within. The city had been keeping it in their museum, unaware of the rarity they had been displaying to the world.

"How do we get it out?" I whispered. Terry, of all people, would be likely to know. He silently gestured to the lock and then to the point of his knife.

"The old fashioned way," he said.

After I had realised that he was in fact being serious, I took it upon myself to keep guard whilst Terry did whatever he did when he picked locks. Many times, the blade of his knife hit the glass, and I was sure one hundred guards or policemen were going to come charging in. The strange thing was that no one did.

Soon, I became suspicious. How could Blue Sea Bay leave their museum with so little security? The answer was, they wouldn't. That left me wondering why exactly Terry and I had been allowed such easy access. Either we had picked the one night no one had been paying attention, or someone in Blue Sea Bay knew we were coming.

I sighed, staying near the door as I listened for any other footsteps. There were so many questions. Unfortunately, the only answers I could come up with were that the people of Blue Sea Bay were either really dumb or that they had sided with Fun City in an elaborate trick of telling us Cleo was captured when he wasn't. I really hoped it was the first one.

I heard a clang behind me and whirled around only to have to glare at Terry, who had let his knife drop to the floor as it opened the lock.

"Can you keep it down!" I hissed at him angrily. Shrugging apologetically, he moved over so I could sit with him. Together, we pulled out the book and set it carefully on the floor in front of us.

"Got any ideas, Kay?" Terry said. I could almost hear the smirk in his voice because I couldn't yell at him for calling me Kay. As it turned out, I didn't have a chance to do anything to him because the book at our feet started moving. Slowly, one by one, the pages started turning. They turned faster and faster until we saw one that said, "You have found me. What do you want?"

We looked at each other and shrugged in unison. To be honest, I think we were too tired and too eager to finish our mission to care that a book was communicating with us.

"We need to use your last wish," Terry said, not sure what we were meant to do.

The pages moved, and we read, "First, you must give me something; then, I will give you what you want."

Terry and I looked at each other. "I don't have anything!" Terry whispered. "No one told us we were meant to give it anything. Did anyone give you anything?"

I tried to say that no one had, but then I remembered my grammie and what she had given me. She had told me I would need it. Slowly, I nodded to Terry and pulled the bookmark out of my pocket.

"First the wish, and then the bookmark," I said, well aware that I was talking to a book.

The pages slumped in what could have been the book's way of sighing, and it turned its pages till it found one that read, "You have one wish left. Use it wisely."

Catching my breath in excitement, I laid the bookmark down on the page and got ready to wish.

"You do it," Terry said. "You were the first one chosen for this thing, and you should be the one who finishes it."

Taking a deep breath, I nodded and stared at the page. "I wish..." I started. "I wish..." But the words wouldn't come out. What did I really wish for? It wasn't just for Fun City's problems to disappear. I wanted to know what was going on. Where was Julie, and was Cleo really in prison? I wanted answers, but I didn't know what to wish for to get them.

"Oh, I wish I knew what I wanted!" I suddenly exclaimed. The book turned its pages till it was closed. Engraved on the back cover was the answer to my wish. "You will know what you wish for from the failures you fix. Bookmark this moment in your life, and you shall have your wish."

Terry looked at me, horrified. "What did you do!" he said to me.

"I...I don't know," I said shakily. "I just...I just...I didn't know what to wish for, and I just exclaimed it, and I didn't mean..."

He sighed, shoulders slumping. "This book was meant to mark something great."

"I know," I said. "I just..." I stopped. "Hang on...bookmark." The way he had said the book was to mark something had reminded me of what the book had said: bookmark. An idea started forming in my head. "I have an idea," I said excitedly.

He looked at me suspiciously. "To do what?"

I looked at him determinedly. "To get our wish back."

But before I could do anything, we heard the sound of footsteps behind us, and we each felt a hand on our shoulders.

2029

If we had known the person behind us was Julie, we would have never whacked her around the head and tied her up with our jumpers. If she had known who we were, well, let's just say I wouldn't be so black and blue.

As it was, none of us knew who the others were. It was only when my torch fell off the glass case and illuminated Julie's face that we realised our so-called enemy was in fact our friend.

"Julie!" Terry gasped, untying her immediately. Though he made haste, we could tell he was trying not to laugh at how she was awkwardly tangled between the arms of our jumpers.

"You could have at least used something softer when you whacked me around the head," she complained as she got up, rubbing her head.

"Well, you got us too," I said. "So we're even." Then we turned serious. "What happened?"

Julie sighed. "That's not completely relevant right now." She looked behind herself into the dark corridor. "All you need to know is that I left the school group and did you a favour by distracting the security guards."

Terry and I sighed in relief. At least we knew Blue Sea Bay wasn't part of Fun City's confusing plan. Julie glanced behind herself at the hazy red corridor.

"Oh, there's one more thing," she said, laughing nervously. "There may be thirty more security guards coming our way."

"What!" Terry and I exclaimed in unison. She sighed.

"Well, you can't expect me to keep the entire security team at bay; there *are* a lot of them."

Terry looked back at me. "You sure you know what you're doing?" he asked, checking.

I nodded. "I'm sure."

"In that case..." Terry picked up his bag and handed the torch and a knife to Julie. "We'll buy you some time," he said, and he and Julie raced down the corridor towards the steadily increasing sound of running people.

Alone in the quiet room, I turned back to the book. I could barely see it, but there was enough red light to help me make out the book and, hopefully, its words.

"All right, Mr. Book," I said. "I want my wish back." I heard the pages turn and held the book up to the light, or lack thereof.

"You have used up your wish."

Unsure whether or not my plan would work, I made my next move. "But you have something of mine, and that means that you have to give me a wish."

The pages turned, and I momentarily wondered how its pages were written with exactly the right answers. Had many people sought the same thing I did? Had they all failed? And did that mean I wouldn't succeed?

"How do you get to this conclusion?" It asked.

I took a deep breath. "My bookmark is in your pages," I said. "A bookmark is something you leave in a book, and it means when you read it, you must start off from that page again. I left my bookmark in you, and now, I want to read, and so you must let me return to the page I left it in."

I literally held my breath, hoping my plan would work. I could almost hear the book sigh as it took in what I had said. Just when I was sure I had lost, the pages started turning, until I was looking at a page that read, "You have one wish left; use it wisely."

Shakily I made my wish. "I wish all of Fun City's mistakes were undone. That all the pollution they've made was gone, and that Atro City didn't have to suffer for all the pollution Fun City made. I wish for a solution to pollution."

All the pages turned, and I was once more staring at the backside of the book.

Engraved in the hard cover was what looked like a poem; it contained the ingredients to make a chemical that would react with the pollutants in the air.

"It worked!" I laughed aloud. "It actually worked!" I couldn't help the smile plastered to my face as I gently opened the book's pages, ready to retrieve my bookmark.

However, before I could pick it up, the pages fluttered until I had another message to read. "You used something of mine; allow me to keep something of yours," it read. If I hadn't known any better, I would have said the book was smirking at me.

"But it's mine! We're even now."

The pages turned once more, only a few times this time. "Let me keep this safe for you."

"But," I protested, "that means I will be able to get another wish..."

The page turned once. "Trust me."

I couldn't stop myself from laughing out loud. The book, the brilliant, amazing book, was helping me! There and then I said to myself that I would apologise to my grammie for not believing in it. It was an amazing object. Quickly, I stuffed it into my bag and ran to join my friends.

The main hall of the museum was in absolute chaos. Glass cases lay smashed on the floor, with guards lying unconscious nearby. I found it hard to believe that the joker Terry and the pretty girl Julie had done all this.

"Quick!" I shouted as I entered the main hall. "Let's go."

Instantly, both of them punched their attackers, and then we burst out of the front doors. Seeing as we had spent the better part of two days running for it, we were pretty good at sprinting our legs off to get away. We made straight for the main street. Surprisingly, we didn't encounter any unwanted attacks, and we concentrated on getting out alive.

The sound of our heavy breathing was loud compared to the still silence of the night. There were no sounds of cars or people to mask the sounds of my footfalls. The City looked empty, reminding me that it was night time, and that we had one day left to get to Cleo and do everything else.

We ran on high alert, well aware that in mere moments, we could easily be arrested. I wondered, for a moment, what my parents would say when they found out exactly what lengths we had gone through to do this. I was pretty sure my mum would freak out. My dad, on the other hand—I thought he would give me one of his proud pats on the shoulder.

Eventually, we saw the city's edge coming closer and closer, and in a matter of steps, we were out of danger. However, we all knew we couldn't stop just yet. We had to get through our own city and make it to Fun City before the end of the day. We had twenty-four hours to give Fun City the book and then somehow find a way to still take the book back to Atro City to use its recipe to stop pollution, get Cleo out safe, get Grandpa Stevenson, and make it back home. So, in simple words, we had a lot to do.

The train wasn't open, as it was barely one o'clock in the morning, so we had no quick transport option to Fun City. Instead, we ran along the tracks, hoping it wouldn't take us too long to get to the other side of our city.

"Here's the plan," I started once we had gotten into a comfortable pace.

Terry stopped. "Wait," he said. "You're not still on about saving Cleo, are you?"

I stopped and turned to look at him, my heart sinking slightly.

"Well, yeah…" I said unsurely. It had been hard to convince them the first time; if they pulled out now, I would have to go through with it on my own. I *was* going to get Cleo and his grandpa, no matter what. "That's why we're running—to get to Fun City," I carried on. Why did they think we were running now if it wasn't to get to Fun City?

Terry and Julie looked at each other and then back at me.

"Kayla," Julie said gently, "we're running now so we can get back to our houses."

My mind imploded. Has your mind ever imploded? Well if yes, then you should understand what I'm talking about. If no, then here's a little help for you. My mind was instantly a whirl of chaos. Parts of me defended my friends, as they had no idea why I had suddenly decided to save Cleo. The other parts scorned them for having so little trust in me. The leftover bits cascaded around, sending me random memories whose sole purpose was just to confuse me. All in all, my head imploded.

"W...what!" I finally managed, once the mental implosion had somewhat receded.

"What about Cleo?" I asked defensively. Once again, Julie and Terry looked at each other, and I wondered just how long they had been planning this moment. How long had they had their minds made up on this?

"Look, Kayla," Terry said, and this was when I knew they were never going to give in. Terry never started with *look* unless he was absolutely sure of what he was going to say.

"You are kind of the one who convinced us not to go back for Cleo in the first place and—"

"That was before I knew!" I exclaimed, realising afterwards that they would enquire about what exactly I knew, and I couldn't bring myself to tell them.

As predicted, they furrowed their eyebrows, and Julie asked, "Knew what?"

I sighed, angrier with myself than with anything. Why couldn't I have just kept quiet and let Terry talk? "I can't tell you right now," I said, knowing it was a poor argument. "You wouldn't believe me."

"Well, maybe you would know if you actually trusted us!" Terry exclaimed angrily, and I couldn't blame him. I had told them they had to help me without a reason.

However, as much as I had expected it, it still horrified me inside when both Terry and Julie turned and made to run down the road in the direction of their own houses.

"Guys?" I called. They momentarily turned, and I took my chance. "You guys can run." I knew that I had been unfair. "But either way, I'm going to do this. I can't leave Cleo." I still wanted them to understand that this was important to me.

We stood silently staring at each other for some time until finally I understood they wouldn't follow me. Heart sinking, I turned and started jogging in the other direction. In my haze of determination, I didn't notice the object that slipped out from where I had hastily zipped up my bag.

The whole running business seemed a lot harder and definitely more boring without the reassuring presences of Terry and Julie. My mind still reeled from the shock that they had left me, so I ran, sometimes unaware of my surroundings.

At times, my mind raged uncontrollably, scorning my friends for having so little faith. I surged forwards, and my surrounding became a blur as white-hot anger coursed through my body.

Then my conscience stepped in. With an annoying resemblance to my mother, it reminded me that my friends were not at fault. My running faltered as I realised it was not them I should blame. Instead, I should blame the fact that they had no idea of my reasoning. It seemed that, from their point of view, I had decided to change my mind for no apparent reason.

However, as a teenage mind does, I answered myself. With a jolt of anger, I realised the true reason for my friend's obliviousness. I became enlightened to the fact that if it were not for their hatred of Cleo, I could have told them my reasons for wanting to save Cleo and his grandpa a long time ago. Once again, I doubled my speed as my mind raged in its ruthless torrent of anger.

However, like my mother, my conscience struck back. I realised that in the event Cleo was unable to defend himself to my friends, I would be the one who should. I realised that it had been my job to prove that Cleo wasn't bad, and I hadn't done that very well at all.

And so it was that I spent the hours until dawn battling with myself about whom to blame. As I reached the train station at the other end of the line, I broke out of my mental battle. As I neared the station, I was barely sure of anything, but one point remained clear in my mind: I had to save Cleo.

Taking a deep breath, I stepped over the border of Atro City. I didn't have the protection of being in my home city or even of being an innocent girl anymore. In Fun City, I was a wanted person. In the minds of the people there, I was a criminal, but I wasn't about to let that stop me.

As I neared Fun City, fog accompanied by a deep chill started to settle around me. I missed Terry's geography knowledge more than ever, as I couldn't see more than a few metres ahead of myself. He would know where we were.

Several times, I tripped over broken tree stumps or narrowly missed walking into long grey buildings. I had to concentrate on simply putting one foot in front of the other as the fog became thicker and thicker.

Finally, I stumbled over a tree root and fell off the curb onto an uneven gravel path. Getting up off my hands and knees, I recognised the road. It was where we had come in the car when we first started our mission.

Now that I had my bearings, I managed to follow the indents made by our very own footsteps, until I once again saw the majestic bronze walls that circled the city.

Since it was night, the walls neither shone nor sparkled. Instead, they looked dark and foreboding as they loomed over me when I walked along them. I was seeking out the small door that I knew was somewhere nearby.

When I was just about convinced I was in the wrong place, it hit me. Quite literally. One of the policemen had opened the door so he could do his nightly round, and as I walked along the side of the wall, I ran straight into it.

"Oi! Pete, what was that!" I heard a shout from inside. Quickly ducking farther behind the door, I pushed my back into the corner, hoping they wouldn't notice me. Luck wasn't on my side—I was noticed straight away.

"Hey, Greg! Get out here! I found 'er. It's the outsmarter lass!" the man said as he roughly grabbed me by the arm. His eyes were hard but shone with glee as he dragged me inside the police house. There, I was surrounded by about twenty policemen, who all smirked smugly.

"Look," I said, glancing discretely around for escape routes in case they didn't listen. "I don't want to cause any more trouble. I'm here for Cleo. I have what you want."

They looked at each other, and finally, one of them stepped forwards. I instantly recognised him as the one who had arrested me the first time. His black eye wasn't the only sign that he never wanted to see my face again.

"That's all good you saying it," he snarled. "But how do we know you won't just run off again. How can we trust you?"

"Well, for one," I said, becoming impatient, "I'm not punching you all, as I should be." Further proving my point, I looked at the policeman behind me and inquired, "Are you sure you want to stand directly behind me?" Hastily, all the men moved until no one was directly behind me. They did not want a repeat of last time.

"Look," I said, "I'm getting tired of this. Either take me to Cleo, or I'll run and take the book with me." They all looked at the man who had stepped forward—he was obviously the boss. They had no doubt in my ability to run and get out on my own, but they didn't know whether I was actually prepared to.

"Take her," the man finally snarled. I was closely surrounded on all sides, and they escorted me out of the building.

From what I could gather, Cleo was being held in the prime minister's mansion. That's where the policemen were taking me to make so I could give the prime minister the book in return for Cleo.

I had expected Fun City to be quiet at night, like the other two cities I had been in. However, despite the hour, Fun City was alive with bright lights and sparkly fountains. It looked as it did in the daytime, only the dirty fog hung lower.

Several times, I had to wrap my arms around myself in order to keep warm. I had stuffed my hoodie in my bag at the museum, a decision that I was coming to regret as every freezing moment passed.

The men took me on a route I hadn't been down before. There were a lot more lights and even people singing on this route. Most of the time, I had no idea where we were, which worried me as it meant I was relying completely on the policemen for directions. Policemen who wouldn't hesitate to knock me out and lock me up right now.

Finally, we emerged out of a tightly packed row of buildings and came face to face with the prime minister's mansion.

"He's at the top," the policeman in charge said. "Dillen will take you there."

One of the smaller guards stepped forwards and pulled me roughly by the arm. "This way," he said.

The inside of the mansion was the same as before, the only difference being the crowds of policemen and guards that littered the hallways. As we walked past, the police men stared at me, and their faces lit up in various degrees of smugness as they saw me finally captured.

I paid no attention to them, save for the one time I glared at a guard who laughed at me. I was too busy trying to figure out what to do next. I hadn't completely planned out how to get out with both the book and Cleo. To be honest, I hadn't even expected to get as far as I had.

Dillen once again pulled me by the arm, and we went into a lift. Smartly silver walls met me as I was crammed in with several other guards. I felt a surge of pride in the fact that they thought I was a good enough fighter to need so many guards.

A metallic *ping* echoed through the lift, signalling our arrival. The guards stepped out and spread, allowing me to see my surroundings.

We were on the roof now. It was as big as a village hall, and we were definitely not cramped for space. Fences lined the gaps on all side so we couldn't fall off, and someone was tied to one of them.

"Cleo!" I said, running forwards. He looked tired if anything but no worse for wear. Before I could get within even a metre of him, I was pulled back by several guards.

"First, the book," one of them said gruffly. Sighing, I bent down and pulled out the book. The guard snatched it out of my hand. Gesturing to another guard, who pulled a table on wheels forwards, he set it down.

"Give me a wish!" he said harshly to the book. Nothing happened. "Open for me...now!" he said, much more harshly, but still, the book refused to open.

Meanwhile, two more of the guards untied Cleo from where he was on the fence. Slightly shocked, he stumbled over to me.

"Cleo! Are you OK?" I whispered to him. He nodded, but I got the feeling he was still too shocked to speak. However, before I had time to say anything more, the guard who had been trying to pry open the book pointed at me.

"It's her!" he said. "She's tricking us. She won't let it open! Take her."

"What!" I exclaimed, edging away from the guards who approached me. "No. I'm not!" I pulled out my knife and stood in front of Cleo. "Stay back!"

I didn't get the reaction I was hoping for. Instead of retreating, one of the guards smirked and instead pulled out a walkie-talkie. "Guards," he said into it. "We need backup. Pronto." There was a moment of static and then the sound of a high-pitched murmur. Then the lift doors opened with another *ping*.

As the doors opened, my heart sank. At least ten more guards were in it. However, before I had the chance to do anything, I saw a bag rise over the guards' heads, swinging around and smacking them all. As the guards stumbled forwards rubbing their heads, a person emerged from behind them.

The last person I thought I would see there.

1983

Barren cracked land—that's the first thing that greeted Lily as she left the gates of Unistate. Fun City, Lily corrected herself. It was known as Fun City now as an insult against Atro City, which would soon have to become her home.

The dry, cracked brown land ran around the gates of Fun City like a moat, but it was less wet. A jungle of long grey buildings followed it—power stations. No matter which direction Lily looked, she saw the grey buildings. In the distance, she could make out some trees, but she had a feeling they wouldn't be there for long.

The car went down a narrow road cutting through the buildings. Wisps of smoke curled up from somewhere on the ground, following the sound of tree cutters.

Lily was driven for around two hours. Eventually, the number of grey buildings dwindled, and they found themselves driving through what should have been green fields but were yellow. Gradually, the car came closer to a blossom of cottages. As they drove past the cottages, Lily could make out the fields beginning to turn greener.

They carried on driving and came to an arch that said WELCOME TO THE ATRO CITY. The space between Atro and City had been widened to emphasise the fact that Atro City was not an atrocity. The driver stopped.

"This is the border," he said. "Get out."

Lily's mouth dropped open. The sandy road carried on for what looked like miles before reaching what looked like a forest.

"You're not going to leave me here!" she exclaimed. "It could take me hours to walk there."

The driver smirked. "Shouldn't have been an Eco then, should you?" he said. He opened her car door, pulled her out, and then drove off, leaving clouds of dust in his wake.

Lily scoffed; Fun City would learn their lesson about polluting soon enough. Looking ahead at the yellowish road, she rolled up the legs of her overalls and began her trek. As Lily neared the forest, she realised it was in the shape of a circle. The road she was on split into two, the left side narrowed into train tracks, which disappeared into the trees and ended somewhere on the other side of the city. The right side stayed as a road, but it circled the city at a far larger radius, meaning Lily wouldn't get any closer to the city by following it. Lily sighed. She was finally looking at her new home.

She carried on walking straight towards what she figured to be the centre of the city; it seemed like a good place to go. Inside the city, people cycled around on sandy paths. Lily assumed they veered off from the main roads at some point so people had some access into the city.

As she walked past people cycling, they stopped and stared at her. At one point, a ginger-haired child stopped and pointed at her name tag. "Look! It's Lily! Lily!" she shouted. Lily stopped and smiled at the little girl.

"Yes, I'm Lily," she said, brushing her dark hair from her face. "How do you know me?"

Instead of answering, the girl shook her head and pointed behind herself. A woman came into view, running down the path with a bike.

"Jenny, slow down..." she said, trailing off when she noticed Lily. "Lily?" she said, surprise etched on her face. She smiled. "Lily, it's so good to see you in person after all these years!"

For a second, Lily thought the woman was mad, but then she recognised the short brown hair. "Willow?" she said in amazement. "Is it really you?"

The woman laughed. Taking Lily's hand, she led her away. "There's much to show you. The others will be very excited to see you after so many years."

Willow knew exactly where she was going. She led Lily down a maze of paths, which was looked over by trees. Her daughter, Jenny, walked with them, questioning Lily the whole way.

"So how's Tyler?" Willow asked. Lily smiled; Willow hadn't changed in sixteen years.

"He's OK. Wasn't happy that I had been caught."

Willow laughed, leading Lily down another path. Houses were built along the path, just far enough away to have front gardens. Lily looked up and realised some houses were also built in trees. "Of course, I wouldn't be happy if my wife got herself arrested either," Willow answered. She patted Jenny on the back, and the girl ran across the front garden of a house. She knocked on the door and was soon allowed in.

"What's Jenny doing?" Lily inquired.

Willow waved a hand. "Oh, that's her friend's house; we were on our way there so she could spend the day."

Lily looked behind and smiled as she saw Jenny's arms waving from one of the windows. That was what Jack would have been able to have had he come with her. In contrast to her previous opinion, Lily thought this little city was quite nice. Although she would miss Tyler and Jack, she was hoping to make a home out of this place.

That was the thing about Lily: she was incredibly stubborn, especially about being happy. She did not see the point in being sad; it just wasted the time she could have spent being happy.

Finally, Lily saw the path open up ahead. As she and Willow neared its end, she saw the path opened up into a large circular shape, with a marble building in the centre.

"This is our village hall," Willow said proudly.

There seemed to be plenty of small paths that opened into the central circle. There was also a rather wide path that led away from the hall, down which Lily could make out shops and a school. That must be the main market street.

Willow took Lily around the hall and down the wide street. They passed the school and several small shops. Finally, they came to a house right at the end of the road.

"Our mischief headquarters," Willow said, leading her inside.

Inside, it was one really big room. The left half was filled with cubicles, each housing whiteboards and pens. The right half was dotted with tables, and there was a small kitchen in the corner. As they walked in, the laughing group around the biggest central table looked up.

"Willow!" one of the men said as he recognised her. He stood up to greet her but stopped when he saw Lily. "Who's this?" he asked, his brows furrowed.

Willow raised an eyebrow at all of them. "Surely you remember our little Laughing Lily."

Lily sighed with a smile. Ever since she had caused a funny bit of havoc nine years ago, she had been dubbed Laughing Lily.

The man stood up straight, as did the others. "Lily?" they asked.

She jokingly flicked her hair. "Of course it's me!" She looked around at the faces of her old friends.

Josh Peterson reached Lily first, brushing his hair out of his blue eyes. "Laughing Lily, it's been a while," he said, hugging her.

Lily laughed, remembering his height and the jokes that had been made of it. "You have the nerve to call me that after the laughs you caused?" She smirked as he turned red.

"Y...yeah! Well...I stopped growing, so HA!" He scoffed. Lily shook her head. Josh would always be Josh. However, as Lily stepped back, she had to admit he had stopped growing. She shook her head in feigned horror.

"What's the world coming to! Josh is right!" she said dramatically. The others also feigned distress but laughed after a minute.

Melanie Walters followed, with her blond hair in a bunch. "I missed you, Lily," she said, smiling at her.

Redheaded Scarlet and her husband, who happened to be none other than Trevor Davies, followed Melanie. Lily looked Trevor over in shock.

"Trevor Davies!" she said with a smile. "Who would have thought you'd be here before me?"

The group sobered. Lily noticed that many of the people had politely left, leaving Lily with her old friends. She turned to the four of them as their smiles faded.

"Why wouldn't I be here?" Trevor asked. His black hair fell over his ears and onto his shoulders, a contrast to his past neatly combed style.

"Why, because you are the prime minister's nephew!" she said.

Trevor shook his head.

"Nephew or not, I was an Eco, and that was enough to make me a criminal in his eyes. He...*disposed*...of me and put my trial on TV, remember?" Trevor smiled and patted her shoulder. "But that is a thing of the past. You, Laughing Lily, are a thing of the now, the latest exile, and our most recent joker." He led her to the table, and a group of around seven other people walked in and sat with them around the table.

"So," Trevor said, with mischief in his eyes. "Tell us what troubles you bestowed on my dear uncle."

Lily sat forwards in her seat. "Well, get ready because this is a good story."

▲

Lily looked around the museum in awe. Light reflected off of every angle in the domed room. The walls were engraved with a honeycomb design. It was as if a giant hollowed-out football had been plonked upside down halfway into the earth.

Walking with a purpose, Lily followed the police instructor into one of the tunnels that led out of the room and into a corridor. The corridor was majestic in itself, housing books and scrolls and giving a tantalising taste of what was to come.

The corridor opened out into another rounded room. This time, the walls were lined with glass cabinets, which were laid out in a circle.

Lily made her way to the middle of the room under the watchful eye of her guard. As she walked, she kept her eyes on the reporters. This was the climax of her plan—her plan to humiliate Fun City.

"Yeah! I agree! It is surprising that the prime minister does this all in secret!" Lily suddenly said very loudly whilst looking at a woman near her as if talking to her. The woman gave her a strange look and walked off, but that was all Lily needed.

The reporters perked up, turning to look at Lily. Ignoring her red criminal's uniform, they held their microphones towards her.

"Breaking news. We have a read on the prime minister's secret activities," one of the reporters said. She turned to Lily. "What news do you have?"

Lily smiled sweetly. "Oh, you didn't know?" she said, feigning surprise. "I thought everyone knew!" She waved her hands as her aunt did when she was about to spill a particularly juicy portion of gossip. "No matter, I will tell you. The prime minister believes in a magic book."

By now, the whole room was silent in shock and watching Lily. Lily mentally smirked; this was going well.

"So here's what I know," she said, leaning forwards.

$$\blacktriangle$$

"And then I told them the biggest bit of nonsense you've ever heard." Lily smiled as the rest of the group laughed.

"That's our Laughing Lily," Trevor said patting her on the back. "Always causing trouble." Lily laughed and raised an eyebrow.

"Well, what do you expect from me?" she asked rhetorically.

2029

"**A**re you OK?" Terry asked me as the guards talked to each other chaotical-ly. They had not seen Terry and were now arguing between themselves about who had hit the guards.

"Yeah…I'm fine," I said. I couldn't believe he was here!

He smiled at my shell-shocked state and gestured for Cleo to follow him as well. "I'll explain it all later," he said. "Right now, we need to get out of here whilst the guards are preoccupied."

Nodding, Cleo followed him, and we all ran to the lift.

"Oh!" I exclaimed, suddenly remembering something.

"Kayla, where are you going!" Terry hissed as I ran back. In answer, I picked the book up off the table, and we finally left the scene.

The cheesy music in the lift was a completely strange experience com-pared to the adrenaline-fuelled chaos of the rooftop.

"You came back," I said, looking at Terry, somewhat unable to believe he was there.

"I did," he said. He pulled a piece of paper from his pocket and showed it to me. I gasped as I recognised it. It was the newspaper I had found at Cleo's father's house. If Terry and Julie had read it, then they knew. "It fell out of your bag as you left," he said. "We read it and decided we couldn't let you do this alone."

"We?" I said. I had seen only him.

"Julie and I." He smiled. "She's planning our escape route."

I grinned back. "Glad you finally saw sense," I joked. He laughed as well and then turned serious.

"You could have told us why you wanted to rescue Cleo. We wouldn't have hated you. You are our friend, and we want to keep it that way, Kayla Stevenson."

After the lift let us out, we ran out the back of the prime minister's mansion, the same way we had gone before. We encountered a few guards and policemen, but the three of us alone were good enough to take them. Well, really Terry and I were good enough, because Cleo could *not* fight.

Once we had gotten out of the mansion, Julie met us by where the annex used to be. "Follow me," she said, bolting the door to the prime minister's mansion closed with a bit of blown-up pipe.

Once we were in the forest, we managed to slow to a walk. The guards wouldn't be able to find us, according to Julie. I didn't know what she had done or how she knew, but I trusted her.

When Julie and I met again, she had said the same thing to me about how I should have trusted her and told her the truth from the beginning. I knew I should have too, and in hindsight, rescuing Cleo and his grandpa was much easier now that Terry and Julie knew why I wanted to rescue them. Grandpa Stevenson was my grandpa, which made Cleo my cousin.

"We're related!" Cleo had said as we all carried on walking. "Just you wait till Granddad finds out! He's been looking for any sign Grandma was alive for ages!"

I had merely smiled. In truth, I was a bit nervous. What was my granddad like?

Eventually, we saw the little cottage in the woods and behind it, a second one. Gladly giving the first one a wide berth, we approached the second cottage, and Cleo knocked on the door. We waited a few moments, and then a man opened the door.

He didn't look as old as I had expected. I had been worried he would be too frail to run as we took him out of Fun City, but he looked as if he could run just fine.

He looked kind, as if he had smiled a lot in the past. The little crinkles around his eyes made him look as if he was even laughing now. Indeed, he broke into a smile when he saw Cleo, but then he saw the rest of us.

He casually looked Julie and Terry over, but upon seeing me, he paled. "Lily?" he said, somewhat shakily.

"No," I said nervously, "I'm her granddaughter."

1985

"**W**oah!" Lily looked within the glass case at the book in awe. Not only had she had the pleasure of visiting Blue Sea Bay for the second time, she was getting to see the famous book of wishes that she had heard so much about.

"It's so...normal looking, isn't it?" Lily looked over at Quint who nodded.

Quint Bains was a runaway from a foreign country Lily had never heard of. He was the one who had arrived with the book in the first place and the one who had hidden it in the museum. Although it had been Josh and Willow who had planned out where to hide it, they had decided Quint should hide it in the museum, as no one would think twice about a foreigner with a foreign artefact, and no one knew him.

"How does it work?" Lily asked. "Because I don't really believe in magic and—"

"It's not magic," Quint said with a smile. "It makes predictions." He stood up as one of the staff walked past them. "I was told when I was given the book that it isn't magic; it only seems like it is. Apparently, the man who wrote the book was thought of as a...prophecy speaker, you could say. He just knew things."

"Like my uncle Hert—he can tell the ending of every movie after the first five minutes." Lily smiled as she remembered the bearded old man.

Quint smiled in response. "Yes," he said, shaking his head. "I suppose you could say that." He paused. "This man, he was similar to, well, you and your Ecos. He saw that our way of life wasn't good for the earth. He predicted

126

what would happen. He wrote the book, not as a magic book but as a recipe book. He wanted it to have the answers to every question and the remedy to every...*wish*—" He said the word *wish* as if it were a private joke.

"But the pages," Lily cut in. "They are said to move."

Quint shook his head. "It is as they say: 'to each his own.' If a person believes the pages can move, then why not."

Lily nodded. It was clever logic.

"I asked the man who gave the book to me a similar question," Quint revealed, "and his answer both inspired and confused me."

Lily's brows furrowed. "What did he say?"

"He said that if seeing is believing, then to see something, you must believe it, and the people who said they saw weird things must deep down truly believe in them. He said, 'I write the answers for people to find; I didn't say *how* they would find them.'"

Lily smiled. She had only known Quint for a few months now, but she was coming to like him very much. He had small brown eyes that were quite close to his nose, which was long and freckled. His black hair was always secured in a bunch at his neck, making his look very wise.

He seemed to have a sort of wisdom she hadn't come across before. There were people who knew facts and people who knew how to make their ways around things, and then there was Quint, who seemed to have a mysterious aura of knowledge around him.

"So how do you get a wish...uh...an answer from the book? What if your question isn't in the book?" Lily asked.

"If you don't believe, then how can you see?" Quint replied with a question and a smirk.

Lily laughed, and Quint's smile faded. "That, and most people end up turning to the page where they have to give something in return for their wish." Lily sighed. So the book asked for something in order to give something; that sounded fair.

Quint turned and made his way towards the exit. "We have to meet the rest of the Ecos at the Dront Café," he said. "We don't want to be late."

"No, you do not." Both Lily and Quint turned sharply towards the voice. One of the museum helpers stood behind them, with a smirk on his face and a walkie-talkie to his ear. Out from his pocket, he pulled a police badge that said Fun City Undercover Protection Agency.

"Found you at last," he said. Almost at once, guards entered the room. A voice crackled from the walkie-talkie, and the man smiled again.

"Your friends are already in our hands, so you may as well surrender."

Lily sighed. This whole I'm-going-to-capture-you thing was starting to get annoying. When would Fun City understand that they weren't going to get their hands on her? And even if they did, she would make more trouble for them.

The two figures looked at each other. Quint raised an eyebrow, and Lily raised two.

Then they ran. Jumping over the glass cabinets, Lily went into the first safe place she saw—the girl's toilets.

She panted as she closed the door of the cubicle behind herself. She could still hear shouting and the sounds of commotion beyond the door. She slowed her breath. She was safe for now.

Ding!

Lily almost jumped out of her skin with fright as her phone gave a loud ring. After hurrying to put it on silent, she read the message. Her mouth opened in dismay. "LL, where are you? We're coming over. Be there in 5."

It was from Willow. If she was talking to Lily, that meant she must not have been caught and that the guard was lying. However, it also meant that all the Ecos were about to come to Lily and run right into the hands of the police. She had to stop them.

Staying as still as possible, she put her ear to the door. It was silent. Taking a deep breath, Lily crept out. The room was empty.

Cabinets had been smashed, and glass was strewn everywhere. Lily ran around the room in a rush. All the artefacts were still there. Noticing something, Lily caught a breath.

Blood.

"Ecos, you are surrounded. We have all of you. Move, and you die."

Lily stiffened as she heard the voice of the guard. Not only had he already hurt someone, he was threatening to kill all the others. Adrenaline coursing through her, Lily ran towards the exit. No one threatened to kill her friends.

Bang!

"Noooo! Trevor!" Someone shouted.

Lily froze as she heard the unmistakable sounds of gunshots. They were followed by a hysterical scream of rage and sorrow.

Bang!

The second shot was followed by a scream of pain. Lily weighed her options. She could run into the scene like a hero and attempt to do the practically impossible, but the whole practically impossible element made that slightly hard.

She had to help from afar. For the second time, she was one of the few Ecos who was still uncaught, but this time, she wasn't going to sit in a cottage for sixteen years like some potato. She was going to help. Turning around, Lily looked at the object. It was time to see how this book really worked.

"All right...come...on...now...yes!" Lily muttered to herself as she picked the book up out of its cabinet. Placing it atop one of the mostly intact cabinets, she sighed.

"Uh...book? Can I have a wish?" she asked hesitantly. Nothing happened. "Is that a no?" she asked. Again, nothing. "Helloooo?"

Nothing. Lily sighed. What she was waiting for was for the pages to move like magic, but she didn't believe in magic. She believed in logic. It was as Quint had said, "If seeing is believing, then to see something, you must truly believe it."

She believed in logic, and that was going to help her see her answer. So, as logic states, she turned to page 1, the place to normally start a book. The top of the page read "Contents." Looking down, Lily saw only one heading listed. It said, "Terms for Wishing—Page 98."

Slowly, afraid that the paper would crumble, Lily turned to page 98.

Welcome to page 98, the terms for the second wish I own.

For my first wish, I asked for a wish in return.

For my third wish, I will ask for something material in return.

So for my second wish, I ask for something equally as binding but not material.

A wish for a nonmaterial item that isn't another wish.

Please write what you will give in the box below.

Lily sighed. She didn't have a pen. Looking around, she noticed a makeup pencil that had been dropped by someone as he or she evacuated. It would have to do. Now for her next problem: what to give.

The book wanted something as valuable as a wish and as binding as a material object. There was only one thing Lily knew that was that special. "A promise," she wrote in the box. Then she noticed a little footnote that said, "Turn to page 109."

She slowly turned the pages.

"Well done, you have been accepted for a wish. Before I fully grant you anything, I need to be sure of what you are going to promise. What is your specific offering?"

There was another box underneath. Lily thought, trying to be as quick as possible.

Bang! Another gunshot.

"I…I…" An idea formed in Lily's head. "Most people would want to find you to see how you work and spread the answer for fame," she said. "I have succeeded. I know how you work, and I know what you are. I am also the one who was interviewed on the news for having released information about you. But here's what I'll do. If you give me my wish, I will give you my fame. I only told the newspapers my name was Mrs. S. anyway. I will not tell anyone, except maybe my closest family members or people who absolutely need to know. The world will not know who used the second wish or how the book works until another person comes along. If you help me get my friends out of trouble and protect them, I will protect your secrets."

Another footnote appeared. "I accept…but know that I will remember your promise…page 678, please."

She turned to the page, happy that her promise had been accepted.

Bang, bang! There were two more shots.

Lily quickly read the page. "What is your wish?"

"I wish that the Ecos get out of this OK and that they can live safely in Atro City. I understand that attacks will be made on us, but I wish that those shot just now will survive and that the rest of us will at least have a fighting chance."

Lily took a deep breath. She could only hope she had done the right thing. Realising that she had finished her wish, she turned to the last page—the logical place to finish a book.

Lying between the cover and the last page was a booklet called *How to Survive the Worst*.

Quickly leafing through it, Lily saw remedies for illnesses and injuries, including gunshot wounds, and also instructions for basic self-defence. She smiled. Now they would literally have a *fighting* chance.

Closing the book fully, Lily noticed something on the back cover. "We shall see each other again. If not through our eyes, then through her future."

She remembered the bookmark Tyler had given her when she had been arrested.

She was now more sure than ever that this bookmark would somehow help her meet Tyler once again.

After placing the book inconspicuously amidst the glass, she turned. She had friends to save.

2029

would have thought that my granddad would want to sit down and chat upon meeting me. Instead, he was instantly up on his feet and ready to get out of the city.

"The longer you are here, the more dangerous it is," he had said. "And I've been waiting too long to see my Lily again."

I didn't want to make grandad run, even though he looked as if he could. I was scared he would get tired too quickly and so walked with him. Terry and Julie kept guard as I became acquainted with my grandpa. He told me about how he had met my grammie, and I in turn told him about everything that had happened to me.

"Your grammie was always a determined girl," he said to me. "We were friends for a long time before we married, and I could never change her mind when she had an idea. It was the same with the rebellion." We passed the clearing, which meant we were halfway home.

"She was the one who took me to where I live now. We used to live in a cottage in the other side of the forest but when she got arrested the first time, she brought me to this cottage. She said she wanted me to be safe. An' usually, it's the men who protect the women, but I had no choice. She's a very determined lady. When she had to leave, I told her to take everything with her. I have barely a thing in my house, just a bed and some kitchen utensils. I'll be glad to leave it all and go back to Lily." I started to see the walls surrounding the city in the distance. "I believe she did the right thing, but she told me to stay behind. She said she would need inside ears. I fed her information for years, but then she just stopped talking to me. I didn't know what had happened or even whether she was alive."

The walls were close now, and Granddad had to pause his story.

"We are going to have to climb," Terry said. "Kayla and I will go first and help you up." He nodded to Mr. Stevenson. "Then Julie will boost Cleo up, and lastly, she will come over herself." We all nodded, and Julie and I shared a smile at Terry and his ever-helpful forward planning.

It was easy to climb over this time as there was no one on our tail. The only hard bit was getting a sixty-something-year-old man over a solid bronze wall.

Julie had helped him from below by boosting him up, and Terry and I had to put more than just a bit of elbow grease into pulling him up from the other side. Eventually, we were all over the wall, and as one, we turned and took in the sight of Atro City.

The sky was blue now, and the sun beat down on the trees in Atro City. It was around lunch time now. The factory was just starting to puff out some stuff as it began work, but none of it was polluting, of course. And of course, in its perfect timing, the train drove up to where Terry, Julie, Cleo, grandad, and I were and stopped.

"Hello, Mr. Haily," I said as we ran up to the station.

"Hello again, kids!" He smiled as he saw us. "Don't tell me you want another ride!"

I laughed, slightly out of breath. "No, no," I assured him. "But you might want to get to the Main Hall; we…uh…have some news."

He laughed aloud. "Ha! You did it! You got the book, didn't you?" I allowed myself a laugh.

"Yes, we did. Now we need to tell everyone," I said.

We half ran down the street and in no time at all, we had passed the white marble church. We wound around the main shopping centre, navigating through carts of food. We spread the news to the shopkeepers who were packing up for their lunch break and stopped to announce our success in the library. Finally, we arrived at the Main Hall, where many had already gotten there before us.

"Granddad…Cleo," I said, "welcome to the finest building in our city."

Then, taking deep breaths, we entered.

Thunderous applause hit our faces. We were ushered to the front of the hall by proud people, all of whom were shouting their congratulations. Somewhere along the line, my granddad was taken by my mother to reunite him with my grammie.

Eventually, we stumbled to the front. Terry, Julie, and I gave each other shocked looks, whilst Cleo grinned from ear to ear, even though he hadn't done anything.

"So," Clinton said once everyone had quieted, "you undertook a great mission and have come back successful." He held up the book for everyone to see. "Our treasure has been brought back to us. These three children have shown great bravery. May their feats be remembered."

He handed the book to Terry who held it up with Julie, and we were met with thunderous applause.

"Wait!" I said, before things could get chaotic. "It's not all over yet!"

"It's not!" Someone moaned from the crowd.

Smiling, I addressed the questioning faces. "No. The book does not simply grant wishes. It's not as easy as that. You may ask it for what you wish, and it will tell you what to do. I asked it for a solution to pollution, and it quite literally gave me one. It has given me the ingredients to make a solution that, when evaporated, will react with the polluting gases in the air. To finally rid ourselves of Fun City's pollution, we must first make the solution. Here are the ingredients..." And so I read out the list of ingredients to the crowd. Faces alight with determination, they worked diligently to gather every one. Soon, Terry, Julie, and I were being approached with ingredients and equipment. Each person also offered his or her proud congratulations, and so our faces were kept suitably red for much of the day.

As evening came, and the solution was evaporated, the whole city gathered outside.

"Five, four, three, two...one!" we cried in unison, counting down to the moment when the solution would evaporate, and our problems would be solved.

The burner was put out, and a thick green fog rose into the air. As it dispersed, we saw the yellow clouds begin to fade away.

Immediately, applause sounded, and once again, everyone applauded for our success. I was so lost in happiness.

Terry, Julie, and I looked at each other with grins. "Well, I could get used to this, huh, Kay." Terry smirked, and for once, I didn't even tell him off for calling me Kay.

1875

Charles had said he would never go back. He'd said that any place was better than Victon, but as Charles walked through the streets of Victon, he thought about what he was coming to do. He chuckled to himself. He'd never wanted to do this, but Lizzie had thought it was a good idea, and he'd learned long ago that annoyingly, when she thought something through, she was usually right. Even if she wasn't, this was the second time he had come back for her, so she must have done something right. Although he remembered that the first time he had come back, she hadn't even known about it.

⋏

Fourteen-year-old Charles sneaked down Tuton Alley. The walls climbed high on either side of him as he stuck to the shadows. He turned onto the main street, looking despite himself at the fifth house in the cramped line, with the same red curtains, that he used to call home.

He assumed his parents lived happily now. He had heard that his mother had had a daughter and that her name was Lucy. He was glad for them, glad that when their son had befriended someone they thought to be a now-dead criminal and run away, they could still be happy. He didn't want anyone to be too sad over him. Running away with Lizzie was his choice. As far as everyone else knew, he had run away, tried to catch Lizzie to turn her in after seeing the truth, and then in the blank relief of her death, he had stayed away.

It was a believable story, but he wouldn't have minded sounding a little more adventurous. He had been the one to believe in a poor person when no one else would and catch said poor person as she catapulted herself out of a window at breakneck speed. But all people seemed to remember was how he had left a shoe behind as he ran. Which, he had said many times, was Lizzie's fault too.

But as Lizzie had "kindly" pointed out, he didn't need to seem adventurous, because her part of the story had enough adventure to cover both of them.

He shook his head. That was Lizzie for you. He turned, making a well-practised leap over the river of filth, to a small shop hidden on the street behind foggy glass and pushed open the door. It was there, where he had seen it two years ago: the object that had started this whole thing.

Letting himself have a sigh of relief, he walked over to the brown book with the shiny cover. He took it to the counter and, with a surge of pride, handed over his five-pound note.

"You took longer than a week," the old lady at the counter said as he handed her the money.

"But I did it," he said happily.

"Wasn't it the girl who wanted it?" the lady asked. Charles smiled.

"It's for her. For her birthday…"

⋀

He could almost remember the day he had run away, the day so much had happened. He remembered the bombs and the police. Had he really done all that? Well yes, he supposed, he had, and much more. He remembered what had started the adventure—his exploration of the wilderness with his best friend, Lizzie, by his side.

He supposed going off to find her parents had started the adventure for real.

⋀

They had been walking for two days. Despite having spent the last day running from everyone and escaping bombs, they were full of adrenaline and ready to find Lizzie's parents. They knew that they lived in Unistate; they just didn't know where.

That's why they were asking around. No one knew anything about where they could be, but when Lizzie saw a street that curved around the outside of the city in the shape of a banana, she just had to try. They walked down the street on the side of the pavement farthest away from the houses, beside the trees and grass, behind which lay the main buildings of the city.

They decided the second house from the end must be the one they wanted. It wasn't an act of fate or a knowing of the heart; it was just painted bright yellow. The bananas and pink roses also helped a bit. Sharing a grin, the duo walked to the end of the road, crossed, and walked in the trees behind the houses until they got behind the one they needed.

Lizzie remembered that as a child, she always used to use the gate in the back-garden fence to get in because she couldn't bear seeing the next-door neighbour. So she decided that she would do the same this time.

Sure enough, as if Lizzie's parents had remembered that Lizzie used to use the back-garden gate, there was a gate in the back-garden fence with a yellow lock that had the very same pin that Lizzie had come up with as a child. She put the numbers in and then walked into the garden.

"How are you going to do this?" Charles whispered to her from behind the fence.

"I'm going to go in, let them know I'm alive, and then…then I'm going to go with you and see the rest of the world, and I'm going to write about all I see and how to solve all the problems," she said. Charles gave her a long look.

"You aren't going to stay and enjoy having parents?" he asked softly. Not that he didn't want her with him when he went exploring, but he didn't want to make her give up her parents.

"No," she sighed. "I haven't been with them for a long time. I don't think I could just stroll in and have it be how it was, not after everything." She saw his face. "I've made my peace with it, Charles," she said softly.

Then she turned and pushed through the gate and walked up to the door. Before she knocked, she heard a cry and slid in front of the window to see what had happened to her mum.

Her parents weren't in the red kitchen, but a mirror was. Looking into it, Lizzie could see into the living room opposite and saw something she never expected. There were her mum and dad, same as she remembered, but with something new.

In her mum's arms was a baby. He was adorable but really tiny, Lizzie noticed, and her parents were looking down at him with love.

"Don't cry, honey," her mother said to him. The baby stopped, and she smiled.

"We need a proper name for you," the woman said. "Something other than *honey*, but the name chart is doing no good."

Then Lizzie noticed the chart taped to the wall next to the window with names they were thinking of. Her heart melted when she saw that each name had the same middle name—El—which was short for Elizabeth. She noticed with a sort of pride that her parents had done as she had: they had never forgotten, but they had made their peace with her memory, as she had done with theirs.

So she turned around, but not before doing something.

"Oh, honey," she heard from behind her. "I thought I saw Lizzie for a minute."

"Well, you could have; she's out there somewhere," came Lizzie's father's reply. "Just because you don't see her, doesn't mean she's not there." Lizzie smiled at her father's logic as she walked out of the back garden and locked the gate behind her.

"Absolutely ri—" Her mother's voice cut off as she noticed what Lizzie had left.

"Oh, darling, she was here!" her mother said in glee. "She gave us a name for the baby. Oh, we love you, Lizzie!" her mother suddenly shouted, and her father joined in as well. She heard the door open as her parents came to see her and quickly ran out of the garden.

"There's no point in me staying, I have to go again. I love you too!" Lizzie yelled back. She knew her parents loved her and that they were alive, but seeing them again would make it too hard for her to leave and go with Charles to write her book. She had lived so long alone and she couldn't just go back to having parents in a split second. They had parted ways and made their peace with that, and knowing one another existed was sometimes enough.

Charles looked at her questioningly. She only shrugged before walking away from the gate. They left as they heard her mother say, "She gave us a name for the baby, dear!" Lizzie grinned; she had written a suggestion.

"It's a beautiful name: Charles El Stevenson!"

𝗔

Charles had been both shocked and honoured. Lizzie had suggested his name! He hadn't understood why until she had told him that he had given everything up for her when he ran, and she was going to make sure that at least his name lived on.

Of course, she didn't know that both their names lived on, that the book she would write would become a legend, or that her brother and Charles's sister would meet and marry and have a son who would move to Unistate and meet a nice girl called Lily. All they knew were their pasts, the pasts they finally remembered.

"I remembered, Charles." He remembered his and Lizzie's conversation under the tree. "I remembered how I got to Victon."

He paused to look at the bookshop that he had visited—five years ago now! Had it been so long?

"I made friends with the next-door neighbour's servant. My father was a doctor, and my mother was a nurse, and so they would often leave me at home, free to talk to him," he remembered Lizzie saying.

He turned the corner and looked down the pathway that led to the rich side of town and the bakery he had said he would buy from.

He remembered Lizzie saying, "My parents were nice, but others weren't. The servant made a daily commute from Victon to Blue Sea Bay to work. He told me about what it was like and the horrors he had seen."

Charles decided in the moment to buy a loaf of bread. His mother would like that.

Lizzie had said, "I told people, starting with my parents. The villagers began to think me mad, and they lost trust in my parents because of it. They wanted me to stop talking. I wouldn't. So they sent me to Victon because they thought it was a nice place."

Charles stepped out of the way of a falling bucket. Victon was a secretive, closed-up town, and so he hadn't been surprised to find out that they were so far behind the times than other villages. His own way of speaking had changed greatly just by having been out of the place.

"Then, it gets fuzzy. I remember a lady coming to fetch me. A horse. The lady fainted on the horse and fell. I fell with her. The horse ran off, and I hit my head on the way down. Then I woke up in the madhouse with no recollection of anything," Lizzie had said.

Charles shook his head. The lady had been none other than Mrs. Edger's daughter, and she had fainted and woken up after having rolled into the cover of a bush after Lizzie had been taken. It was odd how all these years later, the puzzle pieces finally fit together. Lizzie had finally written her book and then promptly lost it after proudly proclaiming to Charles that it was magic. He shook his head. Magic! Not a chance. She had told him that one day it would be known everywhere.

As a book of magic? he'd thought. Not likely.

But he didn't bet on it because he had thought it unlikely that he would ever be here, walking towards his parents' house. He looked at the loaf of bread in his hand and went over the plan in his mind. He, like Lizzie, was not going to walk in and talk. Both Charles and his parents had made their peace with what had happened. He was just here to show them he was still alive, the same way Lizzie had gone to her parents'.

He walked up to the window, smiling when he caught sight of a small girl with red curls sitting on the floor, a book in hand, with her father. He gave a silent laugh and pushed the bread through the window. Then, in the moment, he dropped a piece of paper on top of it. He tapped on the wall by the window and then walked away, blending in with the rest of the people on the street.

"Mummy, what's that?" he heard.

"Charles" was the only answer. His mother didn't call out for him, and he didn't turn back. They had both made their peace now. However, he did stop long enough to hear his mother read out the phrase on the paper bookmark he had slipped in: "We shall see each other again, if not through our eyes, then through our future."

Printed in Great Britain
by Amazon